She Died Unshriven

DAVID FIELD

CONTENTS

SHE DIED UNSHRIVEN

Chapter One

Thomas Lincraft clomped grumpily into the main room of the house in Barker Lane that he shared with his wife Lizzie and their two children, clearly in one of his stern moods. He sat down at the breakfast table and ran his hand casually through his black mop with its first few streaks of grey, clearly indifferent to his appearance, even though he would be on full public display in an hour's time. His wife Lizzie, ever sensitive to his moods, leaned down and kissed the top of his head, at the same time tactfully sweeping several large dandruff flakes from the shoulders of his jacket.

'There's cheese this morning,' she advised him breezily. 'I kept it hidden from the kids, but the milk's gone sour, so it'll have to be small beer. Only one, mind – we want you at your best for the inquest.'

His only reply was a non-committal grunt before he enquired after their two children.

'They're in the grassy ground, playing with that barrel hoop that Robert found; he said that Lucy could play with it as well,' Lizzie advised him as she poured his beer, then took the jug away in case he was tempted.

'See that you bring them inside if it comes on to rain,' Tom instructed her as he cut himself a thick slice from the two-day old black loaf. 'It looks pretty gloomy out there, but not half as gloomy as it'll be *indoors* in the Shire Hall.'

'Please don't pick another fight with the Coroner,' Lizzie pleaded. 'You seem to be determined to annoy the man, and if you want to be appointed as County Coroner's Clerk when Matthew Barton takes his pension…'

'Who says I do?' Tom argued. 'You're the one that wants me to become Greville's lackey. For myself, I'm happy to stay a Constable.'

'Not even the *only* Constable for the County,' Lizzie reminded him. 'There's five of you, and you're not even the most senior of them. But provided you doesn't get up Greville's nose, like you seem determined to do, then we're bound to go up in life, given the number of bad folks you've brought to justice these past years.' Tom's immediate reaction was a snort.

1

'If it means toadying up to that lazy old fool Greville, then I don't want the job, so stop going on about it. It gives me a headache, some days.'

It was the only real tension in the otherwise happy ten-year marriage that had produced two children. Lizzie was ambitious for her brawny, rough cut former carpenter husband to rise above what many regarded as a lowly status in the market town of Nottingham, but Tom had his own deeply ingrained reasons for wishing to dedicate his life to preventing injustice, since he'd seen it in action many years ago, in respect of two of his closest family members. This brought him into frequent conflict with County Coroner Sir Henry Greville, one of two appointees for the County of Nottinghamshire to this prestigious office under the Crown by virtue of the vastness of his estates and the closeness of his friends at the Court of Queen Elizabeth with Keeper of the Great Seal Sir Nicholas Bacon.

Sir Henry regarded this office as no more than his natural entitlement, and clearly resented the many hours that it kept him from his preferred hunting pursuits; in consequence, he was a great cutter of official corners, and took great offence when Tom – who Sir Henry regarded as a nit-picking old woman – insisted on peering into the dark corners of every accusation that was brought to his attention, never concluding guilt until the last vestige of doubt had been expunged.

What made matters worse was that it was not the proper function of a constable to investigate allegations of criminal conduct; a constable was merely required to bring in those accused of crime by others, in addition to apprehending those they saw blatantly committing offences under their noses. Tom had a reputation for pursuing doubts that he should be ignoring if he was to stick to the duties for which he was remunerated.

His frugal breakfast complete, Tom fastened his short cloak by its throat clasp, picked up the staff of office that had rattled many a skull during alehouse brawls, kissed Lizzie goodbye, assured her that he would acquit himself respectfully, and set off down Barker Lane towards High Pavement, from which the sonorous bells of St Mary's parish church boomed out their proud message that yet another nine o'clock communion had been celebrated. He turned into Stoney Street, acknowledging the occasional greeting with a silent nod, and within five minutes he was standing outside the Shire Hall, watching the eager spectators making their way through the open front doors.

The inquest to which they were all attracted was a 'county' matter, so it would be heard in the Shire Hall, rather than the Guildhall, further down at Weekday Cross, which dealt with 'town' matters. He muttered with resignation as he made his way through the front door, then mounted the staircase that led up to the jettied first floor courtroom that was one of the few chambers in the modest market town that could host something as public, and as important, as an inquest.

These were just as much a form of entertainment for those with nothing better to do as the regular Assize courts held in the same courtroom, to which the matter before them today would no doubt be referred by Coroner Greville, once he had achieved the result he appeared to have set his mind on. He would also no doubt, as usual, wish to see it concluded by dinner time, even though Tom retained lurking doubts regarding the formal evidence that they would be hearing.

The dead girl was allegedly one Amy Brindley, formerly a maidservant in the manor house of Anthony Featherstone, the middle-aged hereditary Squire of Lenton Gregory, on the road west out of Nottingham as it headed towards Derby. She had been missing for some weeks, and what was believed to be her body had been discovered, in a woeful state of decay, buried in a paddock on the Featherstone estate, and Coroner Greville had wasted no time in ordering the arrest of Featherstone himself, on suspicion of the girl's murder. This no doubt owed much to Greville's unabashed Catholic leanings, whereas Featherstone was a regular, and highly regarded, 'prophesier' in the 'Dissenter Chapel' in Halifax Lane that Tom also attended, making no attempt to hide his angry contempt for the murderous intolerance of the Church of Rome that had taken the lives of his father and brother during the reign of the former Queen Mary.

The courtroom was already near full, and buzzing with excited conversation, as Tom walked to the side table in order to confirm his attendance in response to the formal summons that had been sent by the Coroner's Clerk, the ageing Matthew Barton, and he was then instructed to take a seat on the bench reserved for witnesses. Across the room were two other long benches, for the jury that the Coroner had summoned to the inquest into the death of Amy Brindley. The fact that only twelve had been called – the minimum number permitted by law – was a further indication that Coroner Greville regarded the matter as cut and dried, and Tom sighed as he took his seat, noting that Greville had cut another corner by summoning townsmen to a county inquest, because it was quicker, although of dubious legality.

A few minutes after nine, the Clerk disappeared through a door behind the 'bench' at the far end of the courtroom, re-emerging only a minute or so later with Coroner Sir Henry Greville in all his finery, his florid face emphasised by the whiteness of the ruff at his neck, and his impressive height increased considerably by the feathered green bonnet. Everyone rose as he entered, and remained standing until the Clerk had announced the formal opening of business, to which he added the traditional – and no doubt compulsory – 'God Save Her Majesty', before inviting those in attendance to be seated. Sir Henry cleared his throat noisily and announced to the nervous looking men on the jury bench that

'This inquest has been convened for today, the Nineteenth day of July in the year of our Lord 1571, in order to enquire into the circumstances of the death of a girl believed on credible evidence to have been one Lucy Brindley, a maid of some twenty four years, whose body was discovered buried on the land of one Anthony Featherstone. Witnesses shall be called, and evidence shall be heard, and it shall be your solemn duty at the end thereof to determine the cause and manner of her death. If it be your concluded opinion that said death may be attributed to the hand of another, then you must not shrink from so announcing, naming that other should it be within your ability to do so. I charge you all, in my capacity as Coroner for the County of Nottinghamshire, and in the name of Her Majesty Queen Elizabeth, to perform your solemn duty without fear or favour, and to render a true account thereof in due course, as you shall answer to God on the Great Day of Judgment. The first witness, Master Clerk, if you will.'

The first witness was George Wolstenholme, Steward to the estate of Anthony Featherstone, a pinch-faced, somewhat haughty, individual who clearly regarded himself as a man of some importance as he stood solemnly in the place designated for witnesses, waiting politely for the questions to commence. Having given his name, age and occupation, he nodded enthusiastically when asked by Sir Henry 'You knew the girl called Amy Brindley?'

'Indeed, sir. She was employed as a general maid in the same household in which I have the honour to serve as Steward.'

'And what were her duties, pray?'

'General in nature, sir, as befits someone of that rank within a properly run house. She would light fires, see to the dusting of the main rooms, and make beds, as part of her regular duties. She would also serve wine and other refreshments on those occasions when the master had visitors.'

'And were those occasions frequent?'

'Not latterly, no, sir, since my master is somewhat advanced in his years, and not given to extensive socialising.'

'Did this Amy Brindley give good service?'

'So far as I am aware, sir. There were never any complaints about her work, if I might express myself in those terms.'

'So had she applied for a letter of good name, you would have supplied her with one without any qualm?' was the Coroner's next question. Wolstenholme seemed somewhat ill at ease when asked this, so Sir Henry pushed a little harder.

'Why do you hesitate, Master Wolstenholme?'

'Well,' the witness replied with a slightly flushed countenance and a pained expression, 'It was only talk among the other servants, you understand, but she was said to be – well, one might say "free with her favours", if I could put it like that.'

'Promiscuous, say you?'

'A rather strong word, if I might be permitted to say so without any disrespect to your good self, sir. But I had occasion to dismiss a coachman who struck my Assistant Steward, and when I enquired as to the cause of their dispute I was advised that Amy had been – well, "carrying on" would perhaps be the appropriate word - with the coachman when the Assistant Steward was under the impression that Amy and he had a – a – an "arrangement", shall we say? Regrettably, it also transpired that said arrangement was of a "financial" nature, if I might express it in those terms.'

The colour rose slightly in the Coroner's face as he stared back intently at Wolstenholme.

'We are both men of the world, witness. Are you saying that the lass charged *money* for her favours?'

'So I was led to believe, sir. I had no personal knowledge of the truth of that, you understand, but . . . '

'Yes, quite,' Greville cut him off. 'But your previously expressed reluctance to supply this dead girl with a letter of good name was as a result of what you had learned of her acts of prostitution?' Wolstenholme went even paler in the face as he nodded. 'Again, a somewhat harsh description, if I might make so bold . . . .'

'This is a coronial inquest, witness, not the swearing in of a bishop!' Greville thundered. 'I need the truth here, as do the good members of the jury who are sitting with me. Did the girl charge money for her sexual favours, or did she not?'

'Regrettably yes, sir. Or so it would seem.'

'Thank you. Now, on another matter, you testified earlier that the dead girl's duties included making beds, is that not so?'

'Indeed, sir,' Wolstenholme smiled, glad to be on more palatable ground.

'Including the bed of the master and mistress of the house?'

'There's been no Mistress of the house these four years and more, sir, since the Mistress Arabella passed out of this life with the sweating sickness that took so many in this part of the country.'

'So your master, Anthony Featherstone, is a single man?'

'A widower only, but yes, sir.'

'A widower is a man without a woman, witness – let us not play with words. I appreciate your loyalty to your master, and it is to be commended, but the fact remains that your master was without a female in his bed. Correct?'

'Correct, sir.'

'But someone who had duties that took her into that bedroom was the believed dead girl, Amy Brindley, also correct?'

'Yes, sir.'

'So the same Amy Brindley who is known to have sold her body to at least one member of the household had official duties in the bedroom of your master?'

'Only domestic duties, sir. I would hesitate to suggest that they were anything other than that.'

'Whether or not they were is a matter for the jury to determine, Master Wolstenholme,' Greville smirked. 'You are permitted to stand down, unless there is anything else you wish to advise the jury?'

'No, sir – I've said all I know about the matter.'

'Indeed, while at the same time advising the jury of additional matters upon which they might wish to speculate,' the Coroner replied with a long stare across at the jury bench. 'Very well, stand down.'

Tom ground his teeth in silent displeasure as he heard the good name of a dead girl dragged through the mud for no apparent reason other than seeking to point the jury towards a finding that would best suit Sir Henry's political and religious bigotry. It was bad enough that the poor girl's future had been snuffed out like a candle, but to blacken her reputation like that with nothing to substantiate it but backstairs tittle-tattle was an unjustifiable additional indignity.

Tom knew only too well how people could be condemned without any opportunity to defend themselves by the merest whisper and innuendo, even from those who had pretended friendship, and sometimes even kinship, with their victims. He pressed his lips tightly together, as if to ensure that his mouth would remain resolutely closed, when he heard the next witness being called. She was the overweight and slightly malodorous lady who had been sitting next to him, taking up more than her fair share of the bench space, and no doubt she was about to kick the tragic girl even harder in her remembrance.

In response to the opening question, the lady boomed out her qualification for being the object of everyone's attention.

'Harriet Marsh, aged forty-three years, widow, and Housekeeper of the Featherstone manor house.'

'And in that capacity you knew the dead girl?' Greville enquired with an encouraging smile.

'Yes indeed, sir – *very* well.'

'We heard from the previous witness his belief that the girl was a whore. Would that accord with your assessment of her character?'

'Most definitely, sir, to the point at which I had complained to the Master regarding her carry-on with the other servants, not to mention others she might be meeting with on her days off.'

'So the Master – Anthony Featherstone – was aware that the dead girl was not above selling her favours for the right price?'

'He most certainly was, sir.'

'And what was his reaction?'

'He did nothing of which I was aware, sir.'

'You mean he did nothing to dismiss her from his service, or to chastise her regarding her immorality?'

'Not so far as I am aware, sir.'

'Do you have any ground for believing that he might have taken the opportunity to avail himself of the same services – the "immoral" ones, I mean?'

'None whatsoever, sir. And if I might make so bold as to say so, I would not have thought that he was given to that sort of thing, sir.'

'But one never knows, does one?' Greville argued with another meaningful stare towards the jury benches. 'A gentleman such as Mr Featherstone would have much to lose, would he not, were it to become known that he was in the habit of dallying with female servants? So he would be anxious to keep that knowledge from you, would he not, along with everyone else in his service?'

'I suppose so, if you put it like that.'

'And if the girl in question – the object of his depraved lust for young flesh – were to threaten to make the matter public, he would have every reason to wish her out of the way, would he not?'

'Again, if you say so.'

'I do not say that this is what happened – that must remain a matter for the jury – but please advise us how long the girl had been missing from her duties.'

Mrs Marsh thought long and hard before replying. 'It must have been a couple of months, anyway.'

'So, since we know that a body believed to be hers was discovered on the third day of this month – July – you would say that she had been absent from her duties since sometime in May?'

'Yes, sir, that would be about right.'

'Was there any speculation, at the time, about why she might have left so precipitously? I take it that she did not give notice?'

'No, sir – she just up and left. There were some who thought that maybe she'd found a better position somewhere else, and some who thought that perhaps . . . well, perhaps, given her Godless life, that she might be in the family way, if you'll forgive me for mentioning it, sir.'

'You must mention everything that you think may be relevant to how she came to meet her violent end, witness,' Greville smiled encouragingly. 'Did she give any ground for believing that her sinful ways might have been her downfall? That they might, as matters fell out, have led to her death?'

'No, sir. It was just the speculation among the household, sir.'

'But if she *was* with child, the person who had got her into that state would also have benefitted considerably from her demise, would they not?'

'I suppose they would, yes, sir.'

'Anything else you can tell us, witness?'

'Not really – except that she was otherwise a most likeable lass, sir. Very open and friendly, like.'

'And possibly very open and friendly with the wrong person. Yes, thank you for your attendance, witness. You're free to leave, should you so wish, as indeed are you, Mr Wolstenholme. I'm sorry, I should have advised you of that earlier. Now, where are we? Yes, I think we have time, before we adjourn for dinner, to hear from the man who discovered the body. Mr Hoskins, would you step into the witness space please?'

So far as Tom was concerned, matters were about to go from bad to worse. It was one thing to hear the good name of a tragically murdered girl dragged through the midden of public opinion, but now he had to sit and listen to a most blasphemous set of untruths from a man who should be ashamed of himself for perpetuating Popish fairy tales among a gullible and largely naive group of his fellow citizens in order to cover up what he had *really* been up to that afternoon. Tom gritted his teeth once again, and kept his eyes on the floorboards as Ben Hoskins gave his full name, announced his age as being thirty-four, and described his profession as that of tanner.

'I believe,' Greville began with an open and inviting smile, 'that you were the one who discovered the body believed to be that of the unfortunate Amy Brindley?'

'I didn't know what her full name were then,' Hoskins began, 'but yes, I found her body right enough, along with others of my acquaintance.'

'Would you tell the jury, if you would, how this came about?'

'Yes, glad to be of assistance, Your Worship. It were like this, you see. I were coming back from a trip in my wagon to Derby, on business, when my horse kind of reared up in its shafts and gave a whinny of fear. I looks up, and there were like this here ghost in the middle of the road I were driving along. "Lenton Lane", we calls it.'

'Did I hear you correctly, witness? Did you just mention a "ghost"?'

'That's right, your Highness. A girl, it were. A young lass maybe in her twenties, no more than that, wearing a blue gown of some sort, looking pale in the face, and with a bright light all around her.'

'So what did you do?'

'I nearly shit myself, to be honest. Sorry, but it's the truth. I were just wondering how to get out of her way when she said something.'

'And what did she say?'

'She said as how her name were "Amy", and she'd been working for the squire of the manor whose land I were passing at the time, and as how he'd done her in because she were expecting his bubby, then buried her in the bottom paddock, next to the road I'd been travelling down.'

'And what did you do next?'

'I got down off the wagon, and followed her into the paddock, like she insisted. I were scared to do anything else, to tell you the truth. It's not often a ghost tells you what to do.'

'Then what, witness?'

'She led me to a piece of ground under a big oak tree, and said as how I'd find her body under it if I dug down a few feet. It looked as if she might be right, because there were a patch of grass what looked different from the rest, so I promised her I'd come back when I had something to dig with, and she kind of smiled, then disappeared out of sight.'

'And did you keep your promise?'

'Yes, but not straight away, mind. I went back into town and called in at the Guildhall and told Constable Lincraft what had happened. I don't think he were inclined to believe me at first, but I reminded him that it were his public duty to deal with complaints and suchlike, and he agreed to come back with me. But first we had to borrow some tools from local folk, and most of them offered to come with us. Then we went back and found the body. Horrible, it were – all shrivelled and stinking.'

'Yes, thank you, witness. I believe that another witness will be describing the body in more detail later. Is there anything else you can tell us?'

'No, that were about it, so far as I can remember.'

'This "ghost" that confronted you – what reason do you have for believing that it really *was* the spirit of the dead girl?'

'Well, for one thing, she were dressed just like the body when we dug it up – the same sort of blue smock, anyway. And of course she'd been able to tell me exactly where she were buried.'

'Yes, quite. And I believe you said that she named her murderer to you?'

'Aye – she said it were the man she worked for – him what owns the big house up at Lenton Gregory.'

'And she told you why he'd murdered her?'

'Yeah – she were in the shit with a bubby what were his. Sorry

11

– my language can get a bit rough and ready sometimes, you know?'

'No need to apologise, witness, since it must be quite an ordeal even recalling those dreadful events. You're free to go now, if that's all.'

Hoskins scuttled back to the witness bench while Coroner Greville was announcing a one hour adjournment for dinner, and everyone made their way out into the noonday gloom. Including Tom Lincraft, who was cursing quietly under his breath.

Chapter Two

Thirty minutes later Tom was still muttering as he sat perched on the lowest of the steps before they met the rutted road in front of the Shire Hall, oblivious to the heavy rain drops that were landing spasmodically on the shoulders of his cloak, and which gave early warning of something worse to come from the leaden skies that had been lowering over the town since daybreak.

A few feet behind him, and set into one of the upper steps, was the gibbet on which were regularly displayed the bodies of those hanged as highwaymen or traitors, allegedly in the name of justice. Fortunately there was nothing on display today, or else Tom would have sat elsewhere, but the mere sight of this gruesome reminder of the cruelty of which 'the established order' was capable brought the nightmare memories back.

Somewhere down south, in a part of London known as 'Smithfield', was a plaque on which were inscribed the names of those Protestants who had been burned to death there sixteen years ago, in the course of the evil and tyrannical persecution ordered by the former Queen Mary, and enthusiastically pursued by her senior clerics. In the case of the true believers of the old city this had been the Bishop of London, and two of the names on the inscription were that of 'Lincraft'. His father Edward and his older brother Richard, mercilessly betrayed by Tom's cousin Francis in return for absolution of his sin of lying with his own sister.

Tom had never spoken another civil word to cousin Francis since Tom, his mother and his younger brother, had fled north and finished up in Nottingham, taken in as an act of charity by his mother's carpenter brother. In fact Tom and Francis had never met since, but were the two ever to come face to face while Tom was armed, he would be likely to end his life on the gallows, after spending its last few months in his own lock-up. He had never forgiven Francis, and never would, but night after night his prayers contained a tearful plea to be relieved of the memory of that day.

13

He'd been kept securely indoors in what had then been the family home in Newgate Street, but this had lain only just round the corner from the execution site, and even locked inside the rear room of the humble house he'd been able to hear the agonised screams and shrieked curses of those condemned. For days afterwards the air in the cramped, narrow streets reeked of seared human flesh, and it must have been then that Tom resolved, as a mere youth of thirteen, that he would never again give credence to anything that emanated from the Church of Rome, or any of its posturing prelates. Even less would he subscribe to Catholic rites, or any of the blind superstitions promoted by clergymen in order to hold their flocks in fearful thrall with tales of Hellfire, Purgatory and the machinations of the Devil.

This included a belief in ghosts, those allegedly earthbound spirits that rose from dank graveyards and river marshes to terrify the living, and urge them back onto the paths of righteousness. They no more existed than did Purgatory, in Tom's opinion, and even though the so-called 'Dissenter' group of which Tom was an ardent member were condemned even by those who followed whichever flavour of the English Church was approved of from year to year, he was proud to be counted among those who regulated their conscience in accordance with the word of God as they understood it from their study of the Bible, and without the intervention of priests who told them what to believe, and what was signified by the mumbled Latin phrases of their blasphemous observances.

He could not, and would not, believe in ghosts, and he was damned if he was going to sit by silently while a Coroner's jury of honest, decent folk were hoodwinked into concluding that Ben Hoskins must have known where Amy Brindley's body was buried because her ghost had confided that knowledge to him. Ben Hoskins, of all people – an incorrigible drunkard and brawler who had tasted Tom's staff across his head more than once over the years. There was one other obvious reason why Ben had known where Amy was buried, and Tom much preferred that explanation to the one that Coroner Greville was clearly urging his jury towards, namely that the girl had been done to death by Anthony Featherstone, whose religious fervour was even greater than Tom's, and who preached the word of God with all the power and simplicity of a latter-day Disciple.

'I thought you'd be coming home for your dinner,' Lizzie chided him from where she stood a few feet away, hands on hips, and cutting into his surly thoughts. 'I saw Peter Baker passing our window, and I was told by his wife that he were on that jury. I was expecting you back at the same time. That were ages ago - have you still got time to come home for some lamb stew?'

'I'm not hungry,' Tom growled, and Lizzie was all set to leave it at that since she recognised the stubbornness in his tone. Then to her surprise Tom opted to explain further, as if unburdening himself of a great weight.

'That stupid bloody Coroner seems determined to see Anthony Featherstone hang for the murder of that girl what were found in his paddock. Bad enough that Greville's a bastard Catholic, while Anthony's aye preaching the truth of God's word to them what's prepared to accept the Lord's good grace, but the only evidence against Anthony is some daft bloody ghost story told by an even bigger bastard what couldn't even lie straight in bed! I'll not see Anthony swing on Gallows Hill on the word of Ben bloody Hoskins and some pretended ghost!'

'But if that's what the jury reckons is the truth of the matter, what can you do?' Lizzie pointed out, in the hope of making Tom face reality and avoid yet another confrontation with the Coroner that would do his future prospects no good.

'What I can do,' Tom retorted as the colour began to rise from the base of his neck, 'is to make sure that the jury learns the truth, and not just Ben Hoskins's version of it! There's a crying need for me to smell out some more facts to put to the jury.'

'But the inquest'll be over by supper time, won't it?' Lizzie objected, but Tom shook his head vigorously. 'Not if I gets *my* way!' he insisted, and Lizzie wished him good luck as she slipped sadly away for home.

There was a lengthy delay once everyone had reassembled upstairs, and as Greville lurched slightly heavily into his seat on the bench an hour later, it was obvious that Her Majesty's

Coroner for the County of Nottinghamshire had dined well at the expense of a swift conclusion of the business in hand. Or perhaps, Tom mused darkly, Greville regarded the matter as so foregone that there was no need for an efficient use of time.

Fully expecting to be the next – and final – witness at the inquest, Tom was somewhat taken aback to hear one 'Amos Bridges' being called into the witness space. He was a grizzled middle-aged man with the sort of dark leathery skin that can only be acquired after a lifetime out of doors, and it came as no surprise to anyone to learn that he was employed as a gardener on the Featherstone estate. He was taken through the formalities, during which he revealed his age to be a surprising sixty-three. He was then asked when he had last seen Amy Brindley. He screwed up his lined face in thought, and replied 'That would have been when I were planting out the late carnations under the front winders of the big house. The Master likes them seeded in the hothouse, then bedded out in full bloom in May.'

'And did you speak with the girl when you last saw her?'

'Yeah, like I always did. She always liked to chat about the plants when she came outside, and that day were her day off, and she were going out somewhere or other. Anyway, she stopped and complimented me on this year's carnations. A fine young lass, she were, and what happened to her were a shame and a sin, so it were.'

'Did she say where she was going?'

'Not really, but it must have been somewhere a way away, because she were wearing her big boots. Real proud of them she were, but they was expensive, so she only wore them on days when she was going into the town, or somewhere like that.'

Something in Tom's brain registered faintly, and he made a mental note of 'boots' for when he had more time to puzzle out what had triggered a thought process in his head.

'And this was a day in May, you say?' Greville persisted, and Bridges nodded. 'I couldn't tell you properly what day it were, but it were the last time I ever saw her.'

'Do you recall what she was wearing?'

'Kind of,' Bridges conceded. 'Them boots, like I said, and a blue smock what come down to the heels of the boots. But no bonnet as I can recall.'

'Did she say where she was going?'

'No, but like I said, it must have been a good way away – maybe the town?'

'Did you see anything of your master at this time?' Bridges thought for a moment, then shook his head. 'No, but then I didn't often see him on warm days like that was. That's why he probably waited a day or two more to borrow the spade, since it came on all cloudy a few days after I'd last seen that Amy lass.'

Greville's eyes lit up with enthusiasm as he picked up the point.

'Did I understand you to say just then that your master borrowed a spade from you a few days after you last saw the dead girl?'

'Yeah, that's right. Come as a bit of a surprise, as you can imagine, the lord of the manor doing his own gardening. And at his age, too. He's not like me – we're about the same age, you see, but whereas I been active all my life, the Master's led a more privileged life, and he tends to puff and blow a bit, even if he's just walking out to the coach.'

The impatience was visible on Greville's face as he waited for the old man to finish reflecting on the advantages to be had from an active life, then raised his hand and subjected the witness to a penetrating stare.

'I want you to think very carefully about this, witness. When your master borrowed the spade, did he give any indication of what he wanted it for?'

'No, not then. He were a bit secretive in his manner, and he just said that he had some digging of his own to do, and that he'd return the spade the next day, which he did.'

'So you have no idea what purpose he put that spade to?'

'Oh yeah, I have. Sorry, only you asked me if he said anything about what he wanted the spade for, and he didn't, like I said. But I saw him using it later that day, when I were on my way home.'

'And what was he doing?' Greville enquired eagerly. Everyone waited in frustration as Bridges screwed up his eyes in concentration, and allowed a good thirty seconds to elapse before replying.

'Well, let me see now. He were digging down in the bottom paddock – the one what we keeps for winter bedding for the horses. I called out a cheery "Good Night", but I don't reckon he could have heard me, because he never looked up. He's a bit deaf at the best of times, and it were beginning to get dark anyway. It'd come over a bit cloudy that day, like I said earlier.'

'This "bottom paddock" to which you refer, witness,' Greville prompted him eagerly, 'is it the one closest to the road that they call "Lenton Lane"?'

'Yeah, that's right.'

'The paddock in which the body of Amy Brindley was discovered?'

'Aye, the same one.'

'Now please think carefully, witness. Whereabouts, in that paddock, did you see your master digging?'

'Just under that old oak tree that should have been taken down years ago. I remember that, because it's got dangerous ever since the worm got into the old trunk, and sooner or later it's going to come down. I were a bit concerned in case it come down while the Master were digging under it.'

'And this was a few days after you last saw the dead girl?'

'Yeah.'

A smile of satisfaction appeared on Greville's face, then he summarised what they had just heard for the benefit of the jury as he fixed them with a meaningful stare.

'So, it seems that a few days after the dead girl disappeared your master – Anthony Featherstone – borrowed a spade from you, and was then to be seen digging around the base of the old oak tree in the paddock nearest to Lenton Lane. The same oak tree under which the body of Amy Brindley was later discovered?'

'Yes,' Bridges replied reluctantly, as the full implications of the evidence he had just given became clear in his own mind. 'But that don't mean . . . .' he began, before Greville pierced him with a glare of challenge.

'Doesn't mean *what*, precisely, witness? Bear in mind that it's for the jury to draw the obvious conclusions from your evidence. Are you admitting that you might have misled that jury, albeit innocently?'

'No,' Bridges conceded weakly, and appeared to be greatly relieved when he was told that he was free to go. As he walked slowly towards the door with a sad, and slightly guilty, look on his face the first dull roll of thunder could be heard from the west. Greville smiled as he addressed the jury.

'Just one more witness, then perhaps we can all get home before that storm hits us. Constable Lincraft, please.'

Tom stood stiffly upright as he acknowledged his name, age and occupation, and was asked to describe the events that had brought him into the case.

'I were down at the Town Gaol, just completing duties for the day, when Ben Hoskins burst in with a most unlikely tale about him having seen a ghost.'

'It's for the jury to determine what's likely and what's not,' Greville reminded him sharply. 'Just give us the *facts* as you recall them, and leave the opinions to those authorised to draw them.'

'The *facts*,' Tom continued without any obvious indication that he felt chastised, 'were that Ben Hoskins were of the belief that if we dug down beneath an oak tree on the estate of Andrew Featherstone, we'd find the body of a dead girl.'

'And what was your reaction?'

'Like I said, I don't believe in ghosts.'

'I meant what did you *do* in response to this allegation?' Greville replied testily. 'I assume that you knew your duty, as one of the County Constables?'

'Of course,' Tom replied grumpily. 'You can ask anyone you like in this town, and not one of them could accuse me of neglecting my duties.'

'So what did your duties require you to do on this occasion?' Greville enquired frostily, and Tom cleared his throat.

'There was a report of a body buried in a field, so naturally I were obliged to follow up on it. But since I didn't fancy digging with my bare hands, I went in search of picks and spades and suchlike. When the men I were borrowing them off learned what they was wanted for, they offered to come and help with the digging, and we set off in Hoskins's wagon and went to where he reckoned we'd find a body.'

'And did you?'

'Obviously, else we wouldn't all be here today,' Tom replied sarcastically, to appreciative titters from some of the jury members that seemed to annoy Greville. 'It were a lass in her twenties, to judge by what were left to be found,' Tom added.

'It's important that the jury get all the information you have available, Constable, even if it may be unpleasant to hear, so please don't spare us the detail.'

'Very well,' Tom persevered. 'We could smell it before we even got down to it, and one of the picks sent up a shower of something cold, sticky and stinking before we realised that we'd dug down far enough. About six feet or so, so someone had gone to considerable trouble to bury the evidence of their wicked act. We scraped back the soil at that level and there were this lass in a blue smock and a pair of boots, with a ribbon of some sort round her neck. It were tied tightly inter the bones what was showing through the rotted flesh, so I reckon she'd been strangled.'

'And what were your next actions?'

'We managed to get what were left of the poor lass into the back of the cart, and brought it into town. It were too smelly to take into the Guildhall, so we left it in the wagon in the side lane, and I arranged for one of the women from town that we use for that sort of thing to come and strip the body. Normally it'd be washed as well, but there didn't seem to be any point this time, so as you know I reported the finding to you, and you authorised for the poor lass's remains to be buried in St Mary's graveyard. On the north side, the Reverend insisted, since she hadn't received her last rites before she died. Seems like you got to make an appointment to be murdered these days, if you wants a decent Christian burial.'

This provoked further titters, to Greville's obvious annoyance, but they were too close to the completion of the inquest, so far as he was concerned, so he persevered.

'What further actions did you take, on my authority?'

'Well, you seemed to be of the opinion that suspicion had fallen onto Anthony Featherstone, on account of what the ghost was supposed to have told Ben Hoskins, so I went to his manor house and told him that he were under arrest on suspicion of the murder of a girl called "Amy". I did so with great reluctance, I may add.'

'No you may *not*!' Greville shouted. 'Your eagerness or otherwise doesn't come into this, unless you wish the jury to believe that you carry out only those duties that accord with your finely developed legal knowledge.'

This time the titters were directed against Tom, who bridled as he fired back the riposte 'No, Coroner, I go by the evidence. The proven *facts*, that is – not the tittle-tattle and prejudice that's led a fine Christian gentleman to be locked away in the Gaol for the past week or two.'

'That's quite *enough*, witness!' Greville bellowed. 'Are you presuming to tell me my job? The duties entrusted to me by no less than Her Majesty?'

'Of course not, Coroner,' Tom replied coldly. 'I just follow the proven facts, that's all.'

'And you consider that the jury do not have sufficient facts upon which to reach their verdict today?' Greville challenged him, to be met with the cool response from Tom that 'There's one very important fact that has yet to be proved.' Greville went red in the face as he fired back sarcastically with 'Perhaps you might wish to advise us, from the depth of your legal knowledge, of what precisely that is, Constable?'

'The identity of the victim,' Tom replied with an arrogant smirk.

'But everyone who's given evidence today has advised us that the missing girl was Amy Brindley.'

'No - and with respect to your office, Coroner – the witnesses who've given evidence today have all *assumed* that the body in the paddock were that of Amy Brindley. For certain, Amy Brindley is missing. For certain the body found in the paddock were dressed in the same manner as that described of the missing girl when she were last seen. But no-one's said for certain that the body's Amy Brindley's. Only some make-believe ghost, if you're daft enough to believe Ben Hoskins.'

'Once again, let me remind you,' Greville shouted, even redder in the face, 'that it's for the fine gentlemen of the jury here to decide who to believe, and who not to believe. It's your job as Constable simply to respond to what you're told by others, not to embark on your own investigations. Surely the testimony given by Master Hoskins is the only evidence we can rely on regarding the true identity of the body?'

'We still need something better than the say-so of a ghost!' Tom objected. 'Something more positive to tell us if the body were Amy Brindley's or not.'

'But the body was too far gone for that, surely? And she's been decently buried for some time now,' Greville argued, suddenly less sure of his ground, and Tom nodded. 'That's the case, but there may be other ways of proving who the girl were.'

'You have further witnesses that you've so far failed to disclose?'

'No – I need to make further enquiries,' Tom smirked back. Greville's face was now a delicate shade of turkey cock as he underlined what that would require.

'If you are to make further enquiries, which is not what you are strictly speaking employed for, then this inquest must stand adjourned, must it not?'

'It must, if we're to do things proper by the law, and find out for certain who the dead girl were' Tom reminded him. 'An inquest is supposed to determine who the dead person were, how they died, and why. We know *how* she died, and you've assisted the jury greatly in coming to a conclusion about who done her in. But we can't do nothing more 'til we knows for certain who she were. And "who she were" will assist greatly in concluding who murdered her.'

The inquest was adjourned to groans of resignation from the jury, and with furious looks from Greville towards Tom, but he had made his point and achieved his objective. Now he had to put his skills to the test, and act way beyond his official duty, in order save a probably innocent man from a terrible fate on Gallows Hill, the designated place of public execution on the northern outskirts of the town.

SHE DIED UNSHRIVEN

Chapter Three

'If Peter Baker puts sand into the next load of flour we buys from him, don't be surprised,' Lizzie grumbled as she came in carrying a large bag of vegetables that she began cutting into small portions to supplement the potage that had now been on the simmer for three days, into which she'd made a point of throwing the leftover lamb from the previous day.

'And why might that be?' Tom enquired from his chair in the corner, staring into space.

'Because it were you what insisted on that damned inquest being put off for a week. Peter's on the jury, as you must have noticed, and his wife Martha could barely give me the time of day when I met up with her at the vegetable stall in Weekday Cross. And instead of getting under my feet while I cleans the house, why don't you take yourself out for a walk or something?'

'It's still raining outside,' Tom reminded her, then wished he hadn't as Lizzie threw the knife down angrily on the battered old worktop and stood glaring at him, hands on hips.

'I *know* it's bloody raining, since I were the one what had to go out in it to get the best of the turnips for the pot.'

'Don't swear in front of the kids.'

'The kids are outside.'

'In that rain? Do you want them to shrink?'

'At least if they shrink, there'd be less risk of them tripping all over your big feet. Ain't you got no work to do?'

'Plenty, but I'm just taking a minute to decide what order to do it in.'

'You'd better have something to show for causing that there inquest to be put off to another day,' Lizzie grumbled as she picked up the knife and continued cutting. 'What was you thinking of?'

'I were thinking of poor old Anthony, in that there Gaol every day, accused of something I don't think he did.'

'It's not your job to decide who's guilty and who isn't,' Lizzie reminded him. That's the job of the jury, not you.' Tom sighed.

'Of course. But they can only decide on the facts what they're given, and Greville's decided for himself that it were Anthony what done it, which suits his purpose, since it'd be one less Dissenter for the world. And a damned fine one, at that.'

'Now who's swearing?' Lizzie grinned back at him. 'And trust you to bring religion into things where it don't belong.'

'It belongs in everything we do in life, as I thought you knew,' Tom replied as he fixed her with a disappointed look. 'If you didn't have to look after the kids on them evenings when I'm at the Meeting House, then you'd know what a fine preacher Anthony is.'

'Does that make him less of a murderer?' Lizzie challenged him. 'You're the first to keep reminding me of all the wicked things they did in them monasteries, before the old King changed the way we worshiped God. You can be a fine preacher and still meddle with innocent boys and girls, or so they tell us when we ask why all them so called holy places was closed.'

'That's just the point,' Tom argued. 'They was houses of sin, right enough, but they was *Catholic* houses. The new religion what me and Anthony follow is nothing like that.'

'Says you,' Lizzie retorted as she took a handful of diced turnip and threw it into the gruel pot over the fire. 'For all you know, your precious Anthony Featherstone took advantage of the poor lass what were working for him, then done her in when it were all about to become general knowledge.'

'You're as bad as the bloody Coroner,' Tom muttered, then apologised for his language before he could be chastised for it. 'He as good as told the jury what they should be deciding, namely that Anthony did the poor lass in because she were carrying his child. And all because some make-believe ghost told Ben Hoskins that were the way it happened. Would *you* believe anything Ben Hoskins told you? I'd rather believe in ghosts than the truth coming out of Ben Hoskins's mouth!'

'Mary Draycott reckons that her mother's ghost visits her house every Sunday,' Lizzie commented, to a derisive snort from Tom.

'It's a pity she don't do the washing while she's at it! Her kids smell of piss all the time, according to Robert. Ghosts are for Catholics anyway, which suits Greville of course.'

'Is this all about your religious differences?' Lizzie demanded. 'Because if so, you're ruining your chances of ever stepping up in life. But leaving all that aside for the moment, what makes you so sure that your precious friend's innocent of what he's accused of?'

'Just a feeling in the guts,' Tom advised her. 'It's all too neatly cut and dried, to my mind. There were a witness called to the inquest – Anthony's gardener – who I never got to speak to, and his evidence were the final sinker, if you start with the prejudiced belief that Anthony's guilty, or with the intention of *proving* that he is. You've got to ask yourself who went out to the estate and spoke to that witness in the first place, because it weren't me. And according to what the man said, you could believe that Anthony were seen burying the body.'

'What does Anthony say to that?' Lizzie enquired, and Tom rose from his seat, walked to the table, embraced Lizzie once she'd held the knife out of harm's way, and kissed her on the forehead.

'Thanks for that,' he said gratefully. 'You've just helped me decide where I'm going first this morning.'

As he walked, head down in order to avoid the puddles that had formed in the ruts of Stoney Street after yesterday's storm, he began to rehearse the questions that he must ask of one of the most inspirational Christians he'd ever known. It would be both painful and embarrassing, but certain questions had to be asked. To divert his mind momentarily he reflected on the matter of the boots that had been on the feet of the dead girl, the issue that had rung a faint bell in his head – always something to which he paid attention when conducting his customary enquiries into any complaint that was brought to him. Enquiries that he was not authorised to make, and which would one day land him in serious trouble. Then it finally clicked into place like the good carpenter's joints that he had been taught to make all those years ago.

Sir Henry Greville seemed determined to bully, or at least persuade, the inquest jury into concluding that Anthony

Featherstone had murdered Amy Brindley because she was carrying his child. But why would Anthony do so somewhere outside, when he clearly had the run of his own spacious house to himself – a house in which the girl was confined by her own domestic duties? And yet the girl whose body had been dug up was wearing boots, and despite what Tom had argued in order to have the inquest delayed, and prevent Anthony from being committed for trial, there seemed little doubt that this body was that of Amy Brindley.

She had clearly set out somewhere, possibly to meet someone, and that someone might well have been the one who had done her in; either that or she had been the victim of a madman she'd encountered as she walked through the estate on her way down towards Lenton Lane. In either case, why should it be thought that her murderer had been Anthony Featherstone? It didn't make any sense that he would have lain in wait for her in open view on his own estate, when he could more easily – and certainly more privately – have done the deed in some dark corner of his own manor house.

Down in the basement of the Shire Hall, the turnkey looked through the flap in the heavily studded oak door, then acknowledged Tom's right to access the dismal, cold and dank cell corridor. He drew back the creaking door on its groaning hinges, and gestured with his head for Tom to enter the cell containing Anthony Featherstone. Tom winced slightly against the smell of unwashed body as he did so, and shook Anthony's hand warmly as he rose in greeting from his iron pallet with its straw bolster.

'I'm sorry you're still here,' Tom mumbled, but Anthony smiled reassuringly. 'You have your duty to perform, Tom, and there can be no exceptions – not even for a good friend, as I can hopefully regard myself in your case. That miserable excuse for a human being that serves my food, when he can remember, tells me that I'm likely to be here for a good while yet. Is that true?'

'Yes, afraid so,' Tom admitted as he lowered his gaze, unable to look Anthony in the eye. 'And that were my fault, I'm sorry. I got the inquest delayed, because there's lots more questions to be asked. By me, that is, even though it isn't strictly speaking part of my job. And I have to start with you, I'm afraid. The way things were going, Coroner Greville was set on getting the jury to send you for trial to the Assizes, charged with the lass's murder.'

'That doesn't surprise me,' Anthony sighed. 'He and I have been at loggerheads for some time now, regarding our religious differences, which of course you share with me. For some reason he seems to have taken it upon himself to investigate Dissenters such as ourselves with a view to reporting them to Queen Elizabeth as likely sources of organised rebellion against her rule. Quite why is anybody's guess, but my own suspicion is that it's in order to divert attention from his own Catholic friends, who may be plotting precisely what he's accusing us of.'

'That's a scandal, and unworthy of even a disgrace to public office like Greville,' Tom protested. 'At first I thought he were just being slack and lazy as usual, but from what you said just now, maybe he's got darker reasons.'

'Almost certainly,' Anthony confirmed, 'so what other information do you require from me?'

'First of all,' Tom replied, slightly red with embarrassment, 'there's the matter of the personal morals of the lass Amy Brindley, always assuming that it's her body we found buried in your paddock, though that's looking more and more likely by the day.'

'What do you mean by "personal morals"?' Anthony enquired. 'You refer to her looseness in matters of the flesh?'

'You knew?' Tom enquired, glad to be relieved of that part of the enquiries he felt driven to make.

'Of course I knew,' Anthony smiled. 'My Housekeeper Mrs Marsh would never shut up about it, and was demanding that the poor girl be dismissed.'

'But you didn't?' Tom persisted, and Anthony shook his head. 'Our Lord, when faced with the harlot who was being stoned in the marketplace, urged the crowd "Judge not, lest ye be judged", remember? He also instructed the girl "Go though, and sin no more". I obviously chastised the girl, and warned her of the road to Hell that she was in danger of walking, but why should I dismiss her? Had I done so, I would have been as guilty as the mob seeking to stone the harlot, would I not?'

Not for the first time Tom was humbled by the man's simple humanity, and the grace of God that was evident in his every thought and deed. Even to *think* this man capable of murder was blasphemy, and to actually accuse him of it a mortal sin. Tom's resolve strengthened to do all in his power to free this wonderful man of even the whisper of sin, but there was still something very difficult that he had to broach with him.

'Your gardener Amos Bridges told the inquest that you borrowed a spade from him, but you wouldn't tell him what you wanted it for,' Tom advised Anthony. 'You can see how that made things look black against you.' Anthony smiled.

'I didn't tell him what I wanted it for because he never asked. But even if he *had* asked, I would have probably been obliged to commit the sin of telling a lie, for the best of reasons.'

'Can you tell *me*?' Tom enquired hopefully, and Anthony nodded. 'Of course, but I must swear you to secrecy, for all our sakes.'

'And what's it got to do with me?' Tom enquired fearfully.

'All of us in the Dissenters' Chapel,' Anthony replied as his face took on a more serious look. 'Mind, I mentioned the attempt by Sir Henry to prove that we are all plotting against Queen Elizabeth?' When Tom nodded, Anthony continued.

'I had heard a rumour that Sir Henry was about to visit houses in the county on some excuse or other of searching for evidence of plots against the throne. Some sort of self-appointed mission on his part to divert attention from Catholic intrigue, as I conjectured earlier. Anyway, as it happened there were things in my possession that it would not have been good for Sir Henry and his ferrets to discover.'

'Are you *sure* you can tell me?' Tom enquired, heart in mouth, and Anthony smiled. 'Of course I can, since you share my religious fervour for the truth, and what I am about to reveal doesn't bear directly on your investigations into the dead girl.'

'Go on,' Tom invited him.

'You have presumably heard of Henry Barrow, since he is

frequently mentioned during our meetings?'

'The philosopher what were imprisoned down in London, simply for visiting another Dissenter what'd been imprisoned by the Bishop of Winchester?'

'That's the man. He also wrote several treatises that are regarded as treasonous, if not heretical, even by those Protestants who pose as true Christians at Elizabeth's Court. The best known of these treatises are alleged to attack the Church establishment, when in fact they simply assert, as you and I believe, that every man must make his obeisance to God in his own way, without resort to an established clerical order of archbishops and bishops. This could be interpreted, not simply as heresy – which it clearly is not – but as treason, since Her Majesty is "Supreme Governor of the Church of England", which puts her at the head of all those clergymen who cannot accept – even in Protestant terms – that every man may make his own direct communion with God.'

'So what's this got to do with why you wanted a spade?' Tom enquired, totally at a loss.

'I had several copies of this man's writings in my house,' Anthony explained. 'They had been printed in the Netherlands and smuggled into the country, and I was reluctant to burn them, since I found them to be such a source of inspiration. I therefore determined to bury them, in an old metal casket that I had. I must admit to a certain cowardice on my part, not wishing to be caught in possession of these writings, and perhaps being imprisoned – or even worse.'

'You was seen burying them, by your gardener,' Tom replied with a smile. 'And to make matters worse, it were not long after the girl Amy disappeared, and in the same place where her body were found in due course.'

'Under that old oak?' Anthony confirmed. 'Yes, that was indeed unfortunate.'

'It were more than that, with respect,' Tom explained. 'That were why I did what I did to get the inquest put off to another day. The jury had just heard that you'd been seen digging under that there oak, and if they'd been allowed to come to a decision that afternoon, you'd now be awaiting trial at the next Assize.'

'I shall always be grateful to you for that, Tom, but how can you use the truth to secure my release?'

'Did you have some valuables in your house, what you could have been burying?' Tom enquired, 'and if so, could they have been buried in that there casket you mentioned?' Anthony frowned.

'I can't ask you to tell a wicked lie like that, Tom – even to secure my freedom.'

'I don't necessarily have to tell a lie,' Tom smiled. 'There's ways of saying things that gives the wrong impression, without actually telling an outright lie. But do you want folk to know that you had treasonous writings in your possession?'

'Obviously not, so I'll leave that matter to your conscience, Tom. I only ask that you don't perjure your own soul simply to save my neck.'

'That may not be necessary, if I can prove that you was digging somewhere other than where that lass's body were buried.'

'And how can you do that?'

Tom knelt down in the dust of the earthen cell floor and drew a cross with his finger.

'This is the oak tree, right?' He then drew a straight line below it in the dust, adding 'And this is Lenton Lane, see? Now, show me whereabouts near that old oak you buried them there papers in the casket.'

Anthony knelt next to Tom and made a mark slightly to the north of the cross. 'There – on the side of the oak closest to the house. I was fortunate to find a soft patch between the roots, so I dug there.'

'And you didn't go back and take the casket out of there later?' Tom enquired eagerly, and Anthony smiled.

'I didn't have time, dear friend, since it was only a few days later when you arrested me, on the order of Sir Henry. I hope you can tell me that this poor unfortunate girl was buried somewhere else?'

'Indeed she were,' Tom enthused, his heart much lighter. He made another mark in the dust, to the right of the oak tree. 'There. If where she were buried could be called the "east" side, you buried your casket on the "north" side. All I have to do now is dig where you told me, and that clears your name. D'yer want me to save them papers what's in the casket?'

'Obviously, but you'll be taking a huge risk for your own safety, if you're caught with them.'

'I won't be,' Tom grinned, 'because they'll be locked safe inside a cupboard we constables has in the Guildhall, where we keeps important bits of evidence. If I get caught with them, I'll have to admit that they got dug up on your land, mind you, and claim that I know nothing about what's written in them.'

'Excellent!' Anthony smiled. 'I'm very blessed indeed, to have a friend like you.'

'I'm the one what's blessed,' Tom assured him, 'to be able to claim the friendship of such a powerful man of God as yourself. I've got to go now, but keep your spirits up, because bit by bit I'm pulling apart the web of lies what led to you being locked away in this terrible place.'

The smile of satisfaction was still on his face as he walked through his own front door in anticipation of his dinner. He was a little puzzled that Lizzie hadn't laid out the wooden boards from which they ate their frugal meals, but the reason for that was revealed when Lizzie poked her head through the doorway from their adjoining bedroom.

'You're needed down at Ben Hoskins's place before you sits down to your dinner,' she advised him. 'Seems that he wants his lad taken up for stealing from him.'

'What, Oswyn Pike, the lad what helped us dig for Amy's body?'

'I don't know his name.' Lizzie protested. 'Just that Ben wants you down there as soon as you can. You'll have to put off your dinner.'

'I'm not putting off my dinner on the say-so of Ben Hoskins, so just serve it up,' Tom instructed her.

'You'll leave it until after your dinner?'

'*Well* after – and maybe not until tomorrow. This afternoon I need to see a man about a spade.'

Chapter Four

Tom was whistling quietly to himself as he crested Zion Hill and looked westwards down the long slope towards the meadows, orchards and streams of Lenton, his destination that afternoon. He could do with a stiff walk after that heavy dinner, and Ben Hoskins and his petty complaint could wait until Tom was well and truly ready. It was over two miles to Anthony's manor house at Lenton Gregory, and the walk back would be a lot more demanding, since it would be mainly uphill, but the rain had finally cleared, and it promised to still be fine and sunny when he walked back for his supper in the early evening, since the light would remain until around nine o-clock, given the time of year.

He cast his mind back to when he'd come down this slope on the front of Ben Hoskins's wagon, with five others clinging to its outer edges as they sat inside it, swaying and bumping through and over the many ruts in the well-worn country track to Derby while the implements they'd brought with them clattered and rolled around their feet. There was something about that trip that was worrying away in the back of Tom's brain, but it would have to wait until he had a spare moment among his jumbled thoughts, since the next step in his investigations promised to be crucial.

Who had taken the trouble to speak to humble estate gardener Amos Bridges, and learn from him facts that almost resulted in Anthony being committed for trial charged with murder? Was Tom merely embarrassed since it hadn't occurred to him to speak to someone so lowly who worked outside the manor house itself, or was he correct to be suspicious of the fact that someone had sought Amos out, and perhaps put words into his mouth through bribery or fear? The only manor employees Tom had spoken to had been the Steward and the Housekeeper, and their evidence at the inquest had not varied from the version of Amy Brindley's duties that they'd reported to him, although he'd been taken by surprise by the references to her character that had been forced out of them by Coroner Greville.

It was high time that Tom spoke to anyone else who might be employed on the estate from who he hadn't yet sought information. Once again he reminded himself of the thin, almost invisible, line between seeking out witnesses for a future inquest and making enquiries of his own. But it was a line that he had occasionally crossed in the past, and this time he felt more than justified.

Amos Bridges was easy enough to find, weeding in a vegetable plot to the side of the manor house. Tom called out to him, and the old man straightened his back, smiled and walked towards him.

'Mr Bridges, I'm Constable Lincraft, one of the County Constables.'

'Aye, I remember you from when you come to speak to the Steward and the Housekeeper. You was at the inquest as well, I seem to remember.'

'That's right, I was. I was wondering how *you* came to be there, though,' Tom replied with the warmest smile he could manage in the circumstances, 'since I never spoke to you when I first come up here.'

'It were someone from the Coroner's office,' Amos advised him. 'An old feller, a bit official like, and he spoke to everyone what works on the estate.'

'Matthew Barton?' Tom enquired as his face darkened in annoyance.

'That sounds about right,' Amos confirmed. 'Like I said, he spoke to all of us except Jane Netherfield, what comes in every week to do the laundry and sewing. She weren't in that day, so that Barton feller missed her. Then me, the Steward and the Housekeeper was told to come into town for the inquest.'

Tom thought quickly, and came to the angry conclusion that Barton had been very selective regarding the witnesses he'd summoned. Those who had testified could all give accounts that tended to suggest that the dead girl had been in an immoral relationship with Anthony Featherstone, whereas there must be others in and around the estate who could give different accounts, and perhaps point the finger away from 'the Master'.

34

'I'm sorry that I might have given the impression that the Master had been burying the poor lass,' Amos cut into Tom's ruminations. 'It were just that the feller from the Coroner asked me if I'd noticed him doing anything unusual about the time that Amy went missing, and I remembered the spade he borrowed.'

'About that,' Tom enquired, since Amos had raised the point, 'you told the inquest that you'd seen the Master digging under the old oak in what you calls the "bottom paddock" – the one alongside Lenton Lane.'

'Aye, that's right.'

'Now, think carefully,' Tom urged him. 'Whereabouts exactly under the oak was he digging?'

'How do you mean?'

'Well, you said you was on your way home when you saw him digging – that right?'

'Yeah – so?'

'So you was coming down that track what I walked up from Lenton Lane a few minutes ago, right? So you'd be able to see the oak, and the Master, and Lenton Lane, right? Now then, were the Master digging on the side of the oak nearest to you, or on the side nearest to Lenton Lane, or to either side?'

'Definitely the side nearest to me,' Amos replied with certainty. 'The Master had his back to me, and the oak were in front of him. That's why he didn't see me coming down from the house, and like I said, he's a bit deaf, so he probably didn't hear me when I called out a "Good Night" to him.' Tom smiled.

'Thank you, Mr Bridges. You can console yourself that you said nothing at the inquest to make things worse for your master, because the body were buried to the *side* of the oak, not at the front.'

'Thank God for that,' Amos breathed with relief. 'It's been on my conscience ever since.'

'And you'd like to do your bit to clear his name?' Tom enquired hopefully, and Amos nodded. 'Of course I would.'

'Well, first off,' Tom replied, 'give me the names of *everybody* what works in the house.'

'Well,' Amos replied as he screwed up his heavily lined brow in thought, 'there's the Steward George Wolstenholme, as you know already, and Mrs Marsh the Housekeeper. Then there's Tom Belton, the Under-Steward, Jim Batley the coachman, Nell Sampson the Cook, and Bessie Helms, what works in the kitchen and scullery. And of course Jane Netherfield, what comes in to do the washing and sewing once a week.'

'And what day of the week's that?' Tom enquired. 'Wednesday,' was the reply.

'You mean tomorrow?' Tom enquired by way of confirmation, and Amos nodded. 'Yeah, today's Tuesday, ain't it, so tomorrow will be Wednesday. She normally gets here about eight in the morning, and she's here all day.'

'Looks like I'll be back tomorrow, then,' Tom smiled. 'And when I does, can I borrow that spade?'

'Don't go getting your clothes all mucky,' Lizzie instructed Tom the following morning as he sat eating his bread and lard. 'Why do you need to dig on Featherstone's land anyway – you looking for another body or something?'

'No thanks,' Tom grimaced at the memory. 'One was bad enough.'

He called in at the Guildhall for long enough to take one of the horses that were kept in the stables at the back for the use of Town officials, then he saddled it up and rode sedately through Weekday Cross, up into Bridlesmith Gate, through the town square and back out under Chapel Bar on his return to Lenton Gregory. When he came back in the other direction he hoped to be carrying a casket in front of him on the horse's neck, which would be far preferable to lugging it back on foot, and there was no way on God's earth that he could leave it at the manor house to be discovered, since for all he knew there was someone in the household who was working with the Coroner to see Anthony Featherstone end his days on the gallows.

An hour later he was seated in the well appointed main room in the manor house, the bright sunlight casting cheery beams across the wood panelling as he was tactfully making enquiries of Under-Steward Tom Belton regarding his relationship with Amy Brindley.

'It's obviously all a bit of an embarrassment,' Tom was telling him, slightly red in the face. 'I'm very fortunate to have kept my position in the circumstances, and George Wolstenholme was most generous and understanding about the whole business.'

'You had no reason to believe that Amy were being disloyal to you with the coachman?'

'Of course not!' Belton protested. 'I thought it was just some special arrangement that Amy and I had. If I'd known she was such a whore, I obviously wouldn't have laid a hand on the girl.'

'But you paid her money nevertheless?'

'Yes, but not for – for *that*. Our relationship was much more natural than that, but not long after we started – well, shall we say "meeting"? – she told me all about her widowed mother in Mansfield who was being threatened with eviction from her cottage after her husband – Amy's father - died, so I was happy to give her a shilling or two from time to time. Not every time we – we – we "did it", you understand, so I never associated the payments in my mind with what we were doing. I got the shock of my life when I discovered that she'd given the coachman the same story, and had been going to it with him as well.'

'Did you do it here in the house?' Tom enquired bluntly, far from being inclined towards sympathy for the man, who shook his head.

'Obviously not, for fear of being caught out. We had our own little spot, in the ruins of the old priory across the Derby Road out there. The place was only closed down for good a few years ago, and the old dormitory that housed the monks still retains its roof. We'd arrange to meet down there after sunset on maybe two evenings a week.'

'And you had no reason to believe that she were taking others there?' Tom enquired cruelly, and Belton shook his head, on the verge of tears.

'Obviously not, and I'm *so* ashamed.'

'The coachman what you had the fight with,' Tom prompted him. 'Did he have the same arrangement with the lass? To meet her in the old priory, I mean?'

'No idea,' Belton replied. 'I'd imagine so, but we didn't get down to that level of detail before the fight broke out between us. He was dismissed, and as I mentioned already I regard myself as fortunate to have retained my position here.'

'As it says in the Good Book, "Go though and sin no more",' Tom replied with an unkind smirk. 'Now, can you tell me where I'll find Nell Sampson and Bessie Helms?'

'In the kitchen, where do you think?' Belton replied, glad to have retrieved something of his dignity from the conversation.

The only person in the steam-wreathed kitchen was a portly middle-aged lady who was stirring a pot full of something or other as if determined to reduce it to broth. Rivulets of sweat were running down her rosy cheeks from the lower hem of her bonnet down to the several folds of her chin, and she frowned as she saw Tom standing hesitantly in the doorway.

'Come in, if you're coming in,' she instructed him, and Tom walked into the wall of appetising steam with a smile.

'Coney stew,' the woman advised him. 'It needs a firm hand if you wants it softened up, and these here coneys ain't all that young. Still, with the Master away I only have to feed the household staff, and they'll eat anything you puts in front of them. You the Constable come to ask about that whore what worked as a maid until she got what were coming to her?'

'That's right,' Tom replied with his second encouraging smile of the day, as he rapidly came to appreciate why the Coroner would not have appreciated what the Cook could have told him about the life led by Amy Brindley. 'Knew her well, did you?'

'Not half as well as a lot of menfolk around these parts,' Nell replied with a sneer. 'She were a right baggage, and no mistake. Off every night to wherever she plied her trade, and no shame. It were obvious that sooner or later she'd pick the wrong 'un to raise her skirts to.'

'So, you don't believe she were killed by anyone here at the manor house?' Tom enquired hopefully.

'I doubt it,' Nell replied. 'The coachman what got himself dismissed for belting Tom Belton had slung his hook long before Amy disappeared, and as for Tom himself, well he's a right wet 'un as he couldn't knock the skin off a milk pudding. He won't even chase the rats out of this kitchen, so I don't fancy his chances of killing a big strong lass like Amy were.'

'What about the Master? Tom enquired tentatively, and Nell turned on him with an angry glare.

'I'll not hear a word said against him, do you hear me? The Master's a fine Christian gentleman what treats his staff with respect. You hear about that sort of thing going on in other households, of course, but not *this* one. That's what I told the Coroner's feller, so if you come in here to get something bad said about the Master, you picked the wrong person, and you can leave my kitchen right now!'

'Do you have any idea how many customers Amy had, and if any of them liked knocking lassies around a bit?' Tom enquired hopefully, and in an attempt to deflate the Cook's wrath, but Nell shook her head.

'She never did anything openly round the house, so we never got to see any of her other gentlemen friends, if you could call them gentlemen,' Nell snorted derisively. 'Bessie reckoned as how she took them down to the priory, what's all closed down now.'

'Bessie Helms, the kitchen girl?' Tom enquired as he looked round the kitchen pointedly. 'I don't see her in here, and I'll need to speak to her as well.'

'Depends whether or not you're prepared to breathe in a dose of the shits,' Nell advised him bluntly. 'It were nothing I cooked, mind, but she's been in her bed for two days now, with a right case of the runs. You'll find her room out the back, above the stable.'

'I might wait until another day,' Tom replied with a grimace. 'In the meantime, what can you tell me about the last time you saw Amy?'

'That were the day she went out and never come back. She come in here for her dinner, and she seemed mighty pleased with herself. Her and Bessie was talking about where Amy were off to on her day off, and there was talk of Amy paying Bessie back some money she owed her. That'd be the first time she'd ever done that, so wherever she were off to, her customer must have been rich.'

'And how were she dressed, can you remember?' Tom prompted her, earning another snort in response. 'All fancied up as usual, with that blue smock she always wore when she were going to it with her fancy men. Maybe it were easier to lift up or something. And as usual she were wearing her fancy boots, which makes me think her man that day were something special. She were even wearing that silver brooch thing what she claims to have been given be some feller in town what were her admirer. The poor bugger probably had no idea what a whore she really were. Pass me that ladle, would you?'

Reluctant to become a voluntary kitchen hand, and even more reluctant to be invited to sample what was being beaten into submission in the pot, Tom made his excuses and left via the scullery door that led onto the back green, where a woman in her mid twenties was hanging items of bed linen on the rope in the sunshine. She smiled invitingly, and he walked over.

'You by any chance Jane Netherfield?' he enquired, and the woman nodded.

'That's me. Are you looking for some sewing to be done? Only you've got a nasty rip in your shirt.'

'Goes with the job,' Tom smiled back. 'The fool what done that got my staff round his head, and right now he's in the Town Gaol for assaulting a constable of the law. That's me – Constable Thomas Lincraft.'

'Well, Constable Thomas Lincraft, come and take a seat on that bench over there while I go and get a needle and thread, and sew up your shirt in exchange for you telling me what you propose to do to catch the swine who killed Amy. That's why you're here, isn't it?'

Ten minutes later Tom was leaning in towards Jane as she deftly sewed up the tear in his shirt, and preparing to ask her what she knew of Amy Brindley. She sighed as she bit off the end of the thread with a 'there you go – all mended, and no charge if you find my friend's killer.'

'She were your friend?' Tom enquired, surprised by both that revelation and the cultured way in which the woman spoke.

'She certainly was,' Jane confirmed. 'My best friend – in fact, just about the *only* friend I ever had, until I met my lovely husband. The people in the house told you she was a whore, presumably?'

'Yeah – that's how everyone seems to remember her.'

'Everyone except me. Did they tell you how generous she could be to people she loved?'

'No – definitely not,' Tom confirmed, somewhat confused by the conflicting report he was receiving. Jane smiled.

'She was definitely a whore, but she had her good side too. She was an orphan, and she'd learned to survive, so when someone like me came along with no idea how to make it alone in this world as a woman, she took pity on me. I'd been brought up in a convent orphanage, where I'd learned to do needlework, wash clothes, and speak correctly, in the belief that I'd one day make a good wife to a freeholder, or maybe even a country squire. Then the convent was closed down, and I found work in a country house just outside Derby, where the Master's son proposed marriage to me after he seduced me and got me pregnant. Then he began beating me, and I lost the baby after one of his more brutal attacks. I ran away, and met Amy while walking towards Nottingham on the road from Derby. We got talking, and Amy persuaded me that men weren't worth it, except for what could be wheedled out of them one way or another.'

'I hope she didn't teach you to go whoring, like her?' Tom enquired, horror stricken by the thought, but Jane smiled and shook her head. 'She certainly offered, but it didn't appeal to me, so she let me share her room in the stables here, doing the washing and sewing for the household until I met this wonderful man who'd just lost his wife to a fever, and needed someone to look after his three children. He works one of the farms on the estate, and to cut a predictable story a little short, we were married last year, and I add to the money from the farm by doing sewing and washing, both here on the estate and elsewhere. But without Amy's natural kindness, I dread to think where I'd have finished up.'

'That's a completely different Amy to the one I heard about from them in the house back there,' Tom admitted, confused by these new revelations.

'They no doubt spoke as they found her,' Jane smiled, 'and I'd be the first to admit that she was no saint. She seemed dedicated to using men, exploiting their obvious weakness in carnal matters, and she could be as hard as the winter frost when it suited her. Some men she actually felt sorry for, like the Assistant Steward of the estate here, but most of them she despised, and if she believed that they were cruel towards other women beneath them, like their wives or servants, then she made sure that they paid her the most. As for other women, if they made it clear that they looked down on Amy because of the life she led, then she'd go out of her way to be unpleasant towards them, and flaunt all the money she made from whoring. After all, that's just a physical – almost animal – thing, and it's what's in your heart that matters. Amy and I understood each other, and we were good friends.'

'I'm trying to find out who killed her, so anything you can tell me about who her regular "customers" were will obviously help,' Tom explained, uncomfortably aware of his rough manner of speech compared with Jane's educated tones. She appeared to think for a moment, then added what she could.

'There was one particular man recently, who Amy seemed to despise more than the others, to judge by the way she spoke about him. Someone from the town, I believe, although as usual I think she would have taken him to her favourite spot in the priory ruins. This man was apparently quite wealthy, but mean-spirited, and he and Amy would often argue about the money he'd give her for her favours. I spoke to her for the last time on the day she disappeared, and she seemed very happy about some scheme or other that involved getting more money from this man. She was very keen to tell me how she was going to be wearing the neckband that I'd made for her, which she was always so proud to wear. If she was still wearing it when you found her body, I'd appreciate getting it back some time, because it'll remind me of our friendship.'

Tom felt a lump rising in his throat as he remembered how a blue neckband appeared to have been used to strangle the girl found under the oak tree, and he shrank from telling this lovely lady the complete truth.

'There *were* a blue neckband round her neck, right enough,' he confirmed, 'but how can we tell if it were the one what you give her? A blue neckband is a blue neckband.'

'Not this one,' Jane assured him. 'I made it specially for her on her birthday last year, and I embroidered her initials on it. "A.B" in gold thread. If that's on the garment, then I'd be very grateful to get it back, as a keepsake.'

'Consider it payment for the sewing,' Tom smiled as he bid her farewell and collected his horse from the stable, chuckling quietly as he nudged it down the drive, then into the paddock on the left that sloped gently down to Lenton Lane, with the large, and elderly, oak at the bottom. He pulled the spade from where he'd fixed it under the bridle leathers and walked towards the familiar oak that brought back some horrible memories. His spirits lifted again as he noticed the paler patch of grass roughly three feet square in front of the oak, and he stood on the rim of the blade, which sank effortlessly into the loose soil as he deployed all his body weight. At the two feet depth he heard a dull thud, and within minutes he had Anthony's casket in his grasp.

He took a while to remount the horse with the casket under his armpit, but eventually he managed the delicate manoeuvre, and after returning the spade with grateful thanks he set the horse's head down the drive, and then out into Lenton Lane, with a huge grin on his broad face.

It had been a worthwhile day. Not only could he now explain why Anthony Featherstone had been digging beneath the old oak, but he believed he had a means of identifying the body buried nearby as that of Amy Brindley.

Chapter Five

Tom looked up from the breakfast table to where Lizzie stood in the bedroom doorway with an accusing look on her face, holding up the shirt he'd taken off the night before.

'It's maybe as well you decided to change your shirt, since you been wearing this one since Easter. I were waiting to sew up that hole in the shoulder, but it seems like you done it yourself. Would you care to mend the hole in Robert's while you're at it?'

'I didn't mend it,' Tom smiled back. 'It were the woman on Anthony's estate what does all their washing an' mending.'

'Well, the next time you go up there, you can take her all *our* washing as well,' Lizzie advised him sarcastically. 'How did you get on up there, anyway?'

'I think I can now prove that the dead girl was Amy Brindley,' Tom smiled back at her, but she shook her head disapprovingly. 'I thought that were already decided at the inquest. Weren't you trying to find out who killed her?'

It was Tom's turn to shake his head. 'You know nowt about how these things are done, so leave the finding out to me.'

'You're not supposed to do things like that, anyway,' Lizzie reminded him, and Tom nodded. 'I'm not supposed to do washing and mending neither, so I'll leave that to you.'

'Leave some of that bread for the kids as well. Anyway, you'll need to call in on Ben Hoskins, because he were round here again while you was out yesterday. He's threatening to report you if you don't arrest that there apprentice of his for stealing from his house.'

'I've got better things to do than answer to Ben Hoskins's beck and call.'

'Then you'd better set about them, while there's still some bread left. And take that tin box with you, instead of leaving it by the side of the bed. I stubbed my toe on it twice already.'

An hour later, inside the Guildhall, he took the key for the constables' cupboard from the Senior Turnkey to whom it was entrusted, and took a deep breath before he opened it and placed Anthony's casket safely inside. Already stored inside were various items that would be offered as 'evidence' at future trials for theft, robbery, rape and coin clipping, but the items he was seeking still smelt as bad as they did when they were stripped from the corpse of a long-dead girl.

He braced himself to investigate in the matted folds of the blue smock, and his hand came to rest on the item he was seeking. He unfolded the blue neckband, then gagged as a minute piece of decomposed flesh fell from it onto the floorboards. His determination was rewarded as the neatly embroidered initials 'A B' could clearly be seen on one end of the neckband, the gold thread slightly soiled, but still visible to the eye. The dead girl was undoubtedly Amy Brindley, but, as Lizzie had reminded him earlier, he still needed to prove who'd killed her. Someone other than Anthony Featherstone, that is. With a sigh he replaced the rest of the clothing from the dead girl, locked the door, returned the key to the man entrusted with it, and sat staring at the neckband.

'That smells disgusting!' fellow Constable Giles Bradbury complained from where he sat in the corner of the communal office, sharpening a quill ahead of making a list of stolen items he'd recently removed from the house of a man now two floors below in the cells. 'Can't you take it outside or something? Better still, take it and stick it under Ben Hoskins's nose, and tell him to take a deep breath. I'm sick of the bastard coming in here, demanding that you look into that stealing what he's accusing his lad of. I offered to look into it myself, but he's insisting that it's got to be you.'

Giles was very much Tom's junior, a fresh-faced, broad shouldered, ginger haired former farm hand who was very popular with the ladies. He was the perfect person to have at one's back in an alehouse brawl, and he all but hero-worshipped Tom, with his quiet intelligence and incorruptible soul. The two men worked well together, and Tom would perhaps include Giles in his enquiries into the death of Amy Brindley should the need arise, but for the time being he was obliged to work alone, since he didn't want to risk Giles being dismissed for adopting

Tom's habit of investigating a crime rather than just reporting it and jailing the alleged offender.

'The next time Ben Hoskins comes in here complaining, tell him to go and piss in his bonnet,' Tom growled. 'And if he wants to know why I'm not available, tell him that I'm too busy investigating a false allegation against Anthony Featherstone what he started with all that nonsense about a ghost.'

'You've really got your teeth inter that business.' Giles observed. 'Can't you just leave it be?'

'No I bloody can't,' Tom insisted. 'I'm not going to be party to the wrong feller being hung. And it's time I carried on trying to find the *right* feller!'

He was already over a mile west of the town, riding slowly past the boundary of the Featherstone estate, when he realised that he'd formed no plan of action, and had no reason to be where he was that he could recall, other than a strong desire to get out of the town and back to where it had all started. Ahead on his right was the fateful oak tree under which had been discovered both a rotting corpse and a casket full of politically dangerous writings, and he reined in the horse and sat staring at it as other horse riders, wagons, and the occasional person on foot passed him by on either side. And that set off another train of thought.

It was highly unlikely that Amy had been murdered here, whatever the time of day, since there was a constant flow of people back and forth to Wollaton, Beeston, Bramcote, and beyond, all the way to Derby. It might be easy enough to bury her here at dead of night, but not to strangle the life out of her even under the cover of darkness, when her screams might attract attention. So where had it been done? From what he'd learned on the estate yesterday, it might well have been in the grounds of the old priory, but even then the removal of the body would have to have been done at night. And whoever it was would have required at least a horse to sling the corpse over, or perhaps a wagon of some sort. And of course a spade.

Suddenly his mind clicked back to something that had niggled at him the previous day, and a light began to grow brighter around an idea that had been subconsciously taking shape ever since the inquest. He found himself reliving in his mind the arrival of Ben Hoskins at the Guildhall, claiming to have seen a ghost, and demanding that Tom organise a search under the old oak. The wagon had been empty, but when Tom had raised the obvious objection that they had nothing to dig with, Ben had urged him on with the insistence that he had a spade available. That had not been enough, as Tom had pointed out, and in the final wagonload that had hastened out of town before the light faded had been three spades and two picks, along with their owners. The fact remained, however, that Ben Hoskins already owned a spade when he had come calling with the unlikely tale of a ghost in Lenton Lane!

Or was it just wishful thinking on Tom's part? He had no love for Ben Hoskins, and he wouldn't entertain for one moment the suggestion that the location of the girl's corpse had been revealed by her ghost. He'd already decided, well before the inquest, that Ben's knowledge of the existence of the corpse was more likely to have been as the result of the evil company he kept, and that Ben might be doing one of them a favour – or had perhaps been earning a disgraceful shilling or two – by inventing the ghost story, but would it not also fit what was known of the matter for Ben to have been the one who did Amy in?

Ben was well known as a violent man when in drink, but who was to say that he wasn't like that when sober? He also had a reputation as a womaniser, and had narrowly escaped more than one charge of rape when he'd managed to persuade, or bribe, some of his equally wicked friends to testify that the victim had been either a prostitute, or so drunk as not to remember what she'd consented to up a dark alleyway. So, all the pieces would fit.

Except the pieces that pointed directly to Ben's guilt, while Coroner Greville was determined to see Anthony Featherstone swing for it. Perhaps Greville knew the truth, and was being bribed or threatened by Ben himself, Tom mused, then shook his head to rid himself of the thought. The two men moved in totally different circles, and Ben was unlikely to possess sufficient wealth with which to bribe Sir Henry. Or had Sir

Henry been the fancy new friend that Amy had been boasting of, who'd done her in when she threatened to reveal his association with her? Tom found himself smiling openly at the thought of being the one to reveal that delightful piece of information, then checked himself. He was here to find Amy's murderer, whoever that might have been, and not to settle old scores.

So where to next? His eyes wandered instinctively to the south – to his left, where the crumbling tower of the former Lenton Priory was just visible over the tops of the trees. He might as well make the trip now, before returning to the estate and asking for directions to the house where Jane Netherfield lived with her husband and family, so that she could positively confirm that the neckband that Tom had wrapped around the horse's bridle, in the hope of killing the smell from it with God's good air, was the one that she had made for Amy.

One could almost believe in ghosts, he told himself as he guided the horse slowly through the grass and weed clumps between the old priory buildings that the moss and ivy were rapidly claiming for themselves. Several crows were croaking their protest as he approached each building in turn, wondering which of them might have been the former dormitory that had housed the monks, and he had almost persuaded himself that the faint echo of chanting was drifting from the largest of the buildings, which had presumably been the chapel in the days when men had idled away their days in gluttony and sexual debauchery contrary to the laws of nature. Then ahead of him, in the grass, he saw something glinting in the sunlight, and he commanded the horse to stop, then slid down from the saddle.

He bent down and picked it up, a silver coloured brooch of some sort, somewhat tarnished after spending some time lying at the mercy of the elements, but with the image of an eagle above a castle still quite visible. Tom turned it over, but there was nothing on the reverse to indicate who might have owned it. Then with a start he remembered something the Cook had said as he'd sat talking to her through the coney-flavoured fog. Hadn't she recalled how Amy Brindley had been proudly showing off a silver brooch she'd received as a "present" from her latest, wealthy, admirer – the one she was heading out to meet on the day that she never returned?

On a whim, Tom looked to the side of where he was standing, at a long, low building that seemed to be connected to the chapel at its far end. He knew nothing about the monastic life, but it would make sense for the dormitory that housed the monks to be connected under cover to the place to which they had to walk, at all times of day and in all kinds of weather, in order to conduct their services of worship. Emboldened, he walked through the brick opening that had presumably once possessed a door before some local farmer had removed it for service in a cow barn or something, and he was in a narrow passageway down which a family of rats scattered before his advancing boots.

There were openings every few feet down this passageway, each of which gave access to what appeared to have once been a room big enough for just a bed. These must have been the individual monks' cells, put to a far from holy purpose by a local whore a few years after the departure of the last monk who had presumably put it to a similar purpose, but now a scene was beginning to play itself out inside his head.

He turned and walked the few feet back to the point at which he'd gained access to the corridor, the place where his horse was grazing happily in the long weedy grass. He confirmed that the spot in which he'd found the brooch lay directly in the path a person would have taken carrying a body over his shoulder, and creating enough movement, when heaving the body either onto a horse or into a wagon, for the brooch to have slipped from the inert corpse, silently and unnoticed, particularly if the deed had been done in darkness. There was every chance that this tiny piece of silverware was the final confirmation that Amy had accompanied her special gentleman friend to their usual place of assignation, not realising that she was about to whore herself into a lonely grave under an oak tree. But he needed to return to Lenton Gregory to have this confirmed.

Back in the estate kitchen he was treated to a frosty stare by the Cook, who was accompanied by a lumpy girl with straggly red hair as they stood together peeling parsnips.

'If you've come for more scandal about the Master, just turn round and go back the way you come,' the Cook instructed him, but Tom stood his ground and smiled at the girl.

'Are you Bessie Helms, by any chance? And if so, are you feeling better?'

'I ain't done nothing wrong, if you're the Constable.'

'I am, and I don't believe you have,' Tom smiled back reassuringly. 'But somebody done something wrong to your friend Amy, and I'm trying to find out who that were.'

Bessie looked enquiringly at the Cook, who nodded over the parsnip she was peeling.

'No harm done, I suppose. But take it outside, and if he tries to get you to say something untrue about the Master, come back and tell me, and I'll give him what for.'

Once outside, Tom gestured to the bench at the side of the drying green where he'd sat talking to Jane Netherfield the previous day, and invited Bessie to sit by his side on it. She still appeared reluctant to talk at all, so Tom began by taking the silver brooch from his pocket and holding it out in the palm of his hand, where the girl could see it.

'Do you recognise this?'

'It were Amy's!' Bessie shouted excitedly. 'She were always showing it off, and boasting that she'd been given it by some fancy feller in town what she were going to make a lot of money out of!'

'By whoring?' Tom enquired, but Bessie shook her head, then went slightly red in the face. 'I won't get in any trouble, right? Only I knew what she were up to, and I didn't warn nobody about it.'

'You'll only get in trouble if you *refuse* to tell me what you know,' Tom advised her in a stern voice, and that seemed to do the trick, as the girl launched into a breathless litany that left Tom even more convinced that he was on the right track.

'Well, it were like this. Some time ago Amy told me about this special feller she'd met, what had lots of money, and were prepared to spend it on her if she let him do things a bit on the rough side, if you gets my meaning. You knew she were a whore, so I'm not telling any tales out of order? Well, she seemed to take delight in telling me all about it when she come back from her trips down to the priory. You knew that's where she took them, right? Well, I haven't had a man yet – not the proper way, anyway - and Amy seemed to find it funny to tell me all about how it's done, what her various men friends liked to do, and how she could always charge them more if it were something special. She were always after money, and before she got her regular men friends she used to borrow off me for her fancy clothes and stuff, except I never got any of it back – she could be proper mean like that.'

'The special gentleman she'd just met?' Tom prompted her, before she could get even further off the point.

'Yeah, sorry. Anyway, a few months back she told me that she'd been inter town for something or other – probably whoring – and she'd met this man in "The Bell" – that's an alehouse, right?'

'Know it well,' Tom replied with a grin, and Bessie continued, seemingly encouraged.

'Well anyway, this feller were well off in some trade or other – leather, I think she said it were – but whatever, he promised her twice as much as she normally got if she'd agree to him doing it a bit rough. She must have said yes, because once or twice she come back with bruises on her face and arms, but boasting as usual about how much she'd got from this new found feller. It were always her day off when she met him – Wednesdays – but after a week or two she didn't seem quite so cocky in her manner, and I asked her if something were wrong.'

'And?' Tom enquired eagerly, and Bessie frowned.

'I were coming to that, weren't I? Seems they'd started falling out about how much money he were supposed to be giving her, and she were thinking of giving him over. But not until she'd made him pay through the nose one last time.'

'And that were the day she went missing – the day she went out to meet him one last time, and the day he probably done her in?' Tom enquired eagerly, and Bessie's face fell.

'Don't you want to know what she were planning on telling him?'

'Not really.'

'Well, I'm going to tell you anyway, because I thought it were

51

right clever.'

'She told him she were expecting his baby?' Tom enquired, earning himself a look of scorn from the girl.

'You're not that bright, are you?

'I'm the bloody Constable, so mind your manners!' Tom fired back, and Bessie lowered her head.

'Sorry, but since she were such a whore, what man's going to believe her when she claims that the baby's his?'

'So what was she going to tell him?'

'That she had the pox, and she reckoned it were him what she'd got it off.'

'And were that true?'

'No idea, but she were going to threaten to go round every alehouse in the town and warn all the girls that he had the pox, unless he handed over lots of money.'

Tom thought for a moment, before conceding that this would indeed be a very strong motive for someone to murder the stupid girl, making a threat like that in an isolated place to a man who liked to play 'a bit rough' at the best of times. But there was something important he needed to find out.

'Did Amy ever tell you this man's name?'

'Only his first name – "Benjamin" it were.'

'Are you sure?'

'Course I'm bloody sure – she were forever going on about "My rich Benjamin feller", an how he owned his own business somewhere in the town.'

'What sort of business?'

'Dunno exactly, but I think it were something to do with leather.'

'Did you tell the Coroner's Clerk all this when he were talking to all the staff on the estate?'

'Yeah, and he said I'd be called to tell what I knew at that there inquest thing. But only the Steward and the Housekeeper were called for, in the end.'

'So you could have told the inquest all about this "Benjamin" feller, and how Amy were meeting with him on the day she probably got herself murdered, but you was never allowed to, is that right?'

'Aye – I thought it were a bit strange.'

'It were more than that,' Tom grumbled. 'But the inquest were put off for a week, and it'll be on again next Monday. Could you and Jane Netherfield come into town, to the Shire Hall, that day?'

'I can only speak for myself, but if it'll help hang the bastard what killed Amy, then of course I will. And I reckon Jane will, too, because she were Amy's special friend. But will they want to hear what I can tell them?'

'Trust me,' Tom assured her as he rose from the bench, 'they'll get to hear what you've got to say whether they like it or not.'

Chapter Six

The smile disappeared from Tom's face only when he was guiding the horse down Bridlesmithgate on his way back into the cluster of houses around St Mary's that was 'home'. But before he could put his feet up ahead of supper being served, there was a call of duty he really ought to attend to if he was to avoid Ben Hoskins causing trouble for him, just at the time when Tom was planning even worse trouble for Ben Hoskins.

It was too much to believe that a ghost had conveniently told Ben where to find Amy's body; that had been obvious from the beginning. Add to that the fact that Ben owned a spade, that he was known to be violent when drunk, and prone to violence towards women, throw in the fact that Amy had, shortly before her death, been immorally associating with a 'Benjamin' who claimed to be a wealthy dealer in leather, and a very clear picture was forming in Tom's mind.

But a picture in his mind would not be good enough. He needed facts, and although he had a good deal more than had been revealed to the inquest jury during the first day, he only had until next Monday to gather together the necessary strands of proof that would at least ensure that Anthony Featherstone was cleared of suspicion. What would be even more satisfying would be proof that the poor girl had been murdered by Ben Hoskins. She may have been a whore, but who was Tom to judge? And hadn't he been set a fine example by Anthony himself, with his Christian obedience to the example set by Our Lord when confronted with a woman being stoned for adultery? Poor young Amy had no-one to ensure that her brutal and pitiful death was avenged unless Tom did what he perceived to be his duty.

His reflections on his duty wrestled with his eagerness to get home and have his supper, but conscience won the day, and halfway down Bridlesmithgate he nudged his horse left towards Pilcher Gate, where Ben Hoskins conducted his tannery business from a squalid yard at the side of his imposing jettied three-storied residence.

'About bloody time,' Hoskins growled as Tom tied his horse to the post and held his breath against the foul smells that came with the man's trade. 'But you're too late, of course, as always. The little bastard ran off when I caught him at it, and fuck knows where he's got to by now – halfway to Leicester, I shouldn't wonder!'

'Does he come from Leicester?' Tom enquired, but Hoskins shook his head.

'Not now – he come from there originally, or so he used to tell me, but he were lodging with an aunt of his in Beeston somewhere before he come to live with us. You might find him there, but I doubt it. Anyway, stay right where you are, while I get the stuff I caught him with.'

Hoskins bustled inside, and Tom took the opportunity, after a couple of deep breaths, to look inside the sagging workshop that Hoskins presumably called his business premises. Tom, as a carpenter before he became a constable, knew next to nothing about the tanning trade, but even he knew that it consisted of converting cow hides into leather by soaking them in disgusting mixtures of dung and urine. But although he looked around carefully, there were no cow hides in sight, and nothing by way of finished leather goods.

'Yeah, trade's been a bit slack these past few weeks,' Hoskins admitted, seeming to read Tom's thoughts as he reappeared in the workshop entrance carrying a small leather bag. 'Anyway, here's the stuff I found in the thieving little bastard's room in the stable back there.'

'He lived with you, right?' Tom enquired, and Hoskins nodded. 'Like all apprentices, it were part of his duties to live on the premises, and mix all the potions for the tanning. But lately he didn't have all that much call on his services, and he were mooning around the house a lot. That's when he must have took all this stuff in this here bag – it were found in his room above the stable, and as you can see it's items of my wife's jewellery. "Ellie", her name is – the wife, I mean. Will you need to speak to her?'

'Later, perhaps,' Tom suggested. 'Right now, it seems I have to go in search of Master. . . .what's his name again?'

'Pike – Oswyn bloody Pike. What sort of name's *that* to give a lad – Oswyn? Mind you, if he were stealing the wife's jewels, maybe he's a bit – you know – an arse fiddler?'

'You want him arrested for *that* as well?' Tom enquired sarcastically, and Hoskins shrugged. 'Please yourself – but you got to find the little bugger first. It's your bloody slackness that led to him slipping away, so find the thieving shit and lock him up!'

'You're late for your supper,' Lizzie complained as she stood in the front doorway watching him tying the horse to the hitching rail that he rarely used. 'And does I have to feed the bloody horse as well?'

'I fed him up at the Guildhall,' Tom explained, 'and since I'm going to need him tomorrow, I thought I'd let him bed down in the back garden.'

'It'll be the first use you've made of that in years,' Lizzie remarked sourly as she walked back into the house, where Tom could hear utensils being slammed down on the table. He sighed and went in, wondering whether or not he'd be punished further for his lateness by way of dry bread and even drier leftover meats.

'Where you been all this time, anyway?' Lizzie demanded as she slopped potage into his wooden bowl, and Tom took his opportunity.

'I been out at Lenton, doing my job, and I reckon I've got enough new facts to save Anthony's neck. Then I did what you been on at me to do for days now, and called in at Ben Hoskins's place, to investigate that thieving what he reckons his apprentice lad's bin up to.'

'And has he?'

'Dunno yet, since the lad up and ran away when he were first accused. That's why I need the horse tomorrow. He's maybe skulking out Beeston way.'

'So, what was you saying about saving Anthony's neck?'

'Well,' Tom smiled triumphantly as he put down his spoon in order to allow the contents of his supper bowl to cool down, and pulled the end portion off some freshly baked bread, 'the

Coroner were trying to make out that Anthony done the lass in on the estate, right? At least, that's what he wanted the jury to decide. Well, as it so happens, the lass were meeting a gentleman friend called "Benjamin" on the day she were last seen, and her favourite spot for doing that were the old priory buildings down the road in Lenton.'

'They reckon them's haunted,' Lizzie observed with a shudder. 'Are you saying that the girl were done in down there, so that her ghost will haunt the place as well, along with all them monks?'

'The only ghost of Amy Brindley that exists is in the mind of Ben Hoskins,' Tom insisted. 'I told you before, I don't believe in ghosts, but I do believe in evil people that are still alive.'

'So what did you learn down at the old priory?' Lizzie enquired, and Tom smiled. 'I found something that belonged to the dead girl, and were probably lost when she were being carried out of there, dead.'

'So you can prove that the girl were at the priory when she were murdered?' Lizzie smiled, 'that's something at least.'

'I can also prove that it were probably her latest fancy man what killed her, then took her body out to the Featherstone estate and buried it under that oak tree, probably late one night,' Tom added triumphantly.

'So all you have to do now is prove who that fancy man were,' Lizzie reminded him with a mocking smirk, 'and are you going to eat that potage or just play with it?'

'I'm going to eat it when it lets me, and stops burning my mouth,' Tom replied, 'and as for proving who the fancy man were, I reckon I'm pretty close to doing that. I'm told by reliable witnesses that his name were "Benjamin", and he were in the leather trade. How many of them can there be?'

'You can't mean Ben Hoskins, surely? I know you can't abide his wickedness, and I know he's been pushing you to arrest that lad of his, but where's your proof? Are you sure you're not pointing the finger at him just to get your own back?'

'D'you really think I'm that mean?' Tom enquired, and was not entirely consoled by the fact that he received no immediate denial. 'Well, mean or not, I've got my duty to do, including my duty to eat this potage.'

'It's not my fault I never know what time you're coming home at night,' Lizzie complained, 'and it's all you're getting, so be a good boy like Robert and eat it all up.'

The next morning, when he reported for duty and announced that he was intending to travel to Beeston, Giles Bradbury was looking glum.

'I don't know where you been these past few days,' he grumbled accusingly, 'but there were a snotty-nosed feller from the County Sheriff's Office here yesterday, asking why you've been neglecting your duties lately. Apparently, there's been complaints from the Coroner, and from Ben Hoskins. And while we're on the subject, there's a stack of complaints about stuff going missing from land down by the Leen River – mainly fruit and stuff. I ain't had time to deal with any of it, and anyway it's your turn down there. I got bitten by a rat last time I were down that way.'

Tom thought quickly. The complaint from Ben Hoskins he could understand, mean-minded bastard that he was, and in any case Tom was on his way to investigate that particular complaint. But the one raised by Coroner Greville was of a different order altogether, and could be an attempt by the man to get Tom removed from office before he stirred up any more complications regarding what Greville clearly regarded as the simple matter of sending Anthony Featherstone to the gallows. Along with the loss of any further authority to investigate the truth behind Amy Brindley's murder, which strictly speaking was not part of his duties anyway, would come the loss of use of the horse he was riding to and from Lenton, and today even further out west, to Beeston. And if all went to plan, he'd need some way of transporting witnesses from Lenton into the town.

He hurried down to the basement of the Shire Hall and demanded admission to Anthony's cell. The man rose with a hopeful expression on his face, and Tom nodded in confirmation.

'I'm now able to prove, as near as don't matter, that the lass were done in at the old priory,' he advised Anthony, 'then buried at dead of night under your oak tree. And I'm pretty close to being able to prove who's guilty of the crime, so chin up. But I need something from you.'

'Anything – just ask,' Anthony smiled back.

'May I assume that you still keep a coach on your estate, since you've still got a coachman?'

'Yes – do you wish to borrow it?'

'Yeah – also another horse, if that would be possible as well. And I maybe might need to hide a young boy on your estate. Not sure about that yet, but maybe he could help that gardener of yours in exchange for his keep?'

'Yes, of course – anything you need. If you let me have a quill and a piece of vellum, I can give you a note to the Steward, advising him that you have total authority over the estate in my absence.'

'I don't have time,' Tom replied, 'but thanks anyway. I got to be going now, but with a bit of luck you'll be out of here within the next week.'

Three hours later, having made discreet enquiries in the two main streets of the village of Beeston, four miles to the west of the town, Tom slipped from his horse at the front fence of the cottage in Manor Lane, hitched him to the rail, drew his staff and pushed open the front garden gate. A young man was hoeing between two lines of vegetables, and he looked up in apprehension as he saw Tom walking towards him with a raised weapon. Tom smiled reassuringly.

'Oswyn Pike? I'm told that this is your aunt's house, so you must be him. You've got nothing to fear from me unless you try to make a run for it, in which case you'll get this lump of wood round your head. I don't believe you stole from Ben Hoskins, but there's some information I needs from you.'

'You're the Constable, ain't you?' Oswyn frowned back suspiciously. 'I remember you from when we dug up that body.'

'And that's what I want to talk to you about.'

'*I* never done it!' Oswyn all but shrieked, and Tom gave him a reassuring grin. 'If I thought you had, believe me I wouldn't have just walked through your gate – I'd have kicked it down, then smacked you over the head and tied your hands together. I'd also have brought a couple more fellers with me.'

'So, what d'you want to know?'

'Simple. The day we found that body, when did Ben Hoskins set off from his tannery, and where were he off to?' Oswyn thought for a moment before replying.

'After breakfast it were, but not for some time after. I thought it were odd, because he said he were off to Derby to get some cow hides for the tannery.'

'And what were odd about that, exactly?' Tom enquired hopefully.

'Well, for one thing we hadn't done any business for a week or two, and I don't reckon the Master could have had any money to buy new hides. He always paid for new hides from money he'd made from the last lot of finished leather, and there hadn't been any sales for a week or two. I had no work to do, and was just sitting around the place making myself useful – tidying up the tanning shed and suchlike.'

'And the second thing that were odd?' Tom persisted.

'Well, when he were going to Derby he normally set off at daybreak. I know it takes four hours to get there, because I been with him a couple of times. Then he wouldn't get back 'til supper time, but that day he were back not long after dinner, as you know yourself. So I don't reckon he'd been anywhere near Derby, to tell you the honest truth.'

'So how long were he gone, altogether?'

'Maybe four or five hours – no more than that, anyway, then when he *did* come back, it were with you.'

'So he didn't come back with any cow hides before coming back with me?'

'No.'

'Well there were nothing in the wagon when he called me out to dig for the body, so where do you reckon he might have been?'

'No idea,' Oswyn shrugged. 'But that were nothing unusual for him in them days. He'd taken to disappearing without telling me where he were going. It always seemed to be on a Wednesday, and I reckoned as how he'd taken to gambling, because he never seemed to have any money. He hadn't paid me for weeks, and the meals were getting smaller and smaller.

I reckon he accused me of stealing as an excuse to get rid of me.'

'About that,' Tom smiled, 'Like I said, I don't think you stole anything at all, but tell me how it come about that you was accused of it.'

'It were a fix,' Oswyn replied with a grimace. 'I were cleaning out the shed for the sake of something to do when he comes racing in with a bag of some sort that he claimed had some of his wife's jewels in, and reckoned he'd found it under my bedding in the loft where I used to sleep. It were a ridiculous lie, but he insisted that he were going to call in the constables, and I got scared, because it were just his word against mine, so I ran off, and now you've found me. I ain't done nowt against him, so why would he accuse me of something I ain't done?'

'That's easy explained,' Tom smiled. 'He wanted you safely locked up, out of the way, because of something you know that he don't want anybody else to know.'

'Like what?'

'That's what I'm here to find out,' Tom advised him. 'And I reckon it might have something to do with that spade of his, and one time when he went missing, taking the spade with him.'

'That makes sense!' Oswyn enthused, 'and it explains why he blamed me for losing it!'

'Go on,' Tom urged him, and Oswyn's face took on a reflective expression as he recalled the events in question.

'It were some time ago now, but there were one night when he come home real late. My room were in the loft above the stable, and I were still dozing off when I heard him stabling the horse and cursing really loud. I reckoned he'd lost a lot of money at the cards or whatever, so the next day I kept my head down, because he could get a bit rough when he were in a bad mood – just ask his missus. Anyway, I spent the day cleaning out some of the last of the cow shit what we hadn't used, and putting it into the pile at the back of the yard, using the spade what we kept for that. Then the next night he were gone again, and the following morning I went looking for the spade, because I still had some shit left to shovel out of the shed. I couldn't find it, and then the Master lifted it out the wagon and give me a right telling off for leaving it in there, except I hadn't, see? I just put it down to the fact that he'd lost all his money gambling, and were expecting him to beat either his missus or me, which he normally did when things weren't going right for him. But not this time, because he seemed to have his mind on something else.'

'And when were this, as rightly as you can remember?' Tom enquired eagerly, but Oswyn looked blank until prompted further. 'Were it before the day we found the body?' Tom demanded impatiently.

'Oh yeah, a long time before that,' Oswyn confirmed. 'Maybe a couple of months before then?'

'So sometime in May, you reckon?'

'Yeah, about then. Does that help you?'

'It certainly does,' Tom smiled, 'but it don't help you much, because you're going to be looking for a new trade.'

'Can't I just stay here with my Auntie?'

'You could, once you've told the Coroner what you just told me. But before that, you've got to go into hiding somewhere. I found you too easily out here in Beeston, and Hoskins might come looking for you as well, so how do you fancy doing a bit of gardening work out on a big estate in Lenton?'

'If you says so, but can I finish this weeding before I goes? And do you want to stay for your dinner?'

It was mid afternoon before the two of them left Beeston, with Oswyn perched uncomfortably on the neck of Tom's horse as he walked him carefully along the track that joined the Derby Road at Wollaton, then up the final mile to Lenton Gregory, where Tom dropped Oswyn off with instructions to Amos Bridges that he had a new lad to help him with the estate gardening, on the orders of the Master. Then Tom persuaded the coachman that the spare horse had been loaned to him by Featherstone, and set off for home, after declining the offer of an early supper. He was leading the spare horse by the bridle as he entered Low Pavement at the foot of Bridlesmithgate, and turned towards the Guildhall in Weekday Cross, where a group of armed men were waiting for him.

Chapter Seven

'Am I being arrested?' Tom enquired as he opted to remain in the saddle in response to the apparent leader of the group stepping towards him.

'Thomas Lincraft?' the man enquired, and Tom nodded. 'You must know that, since your face's familiar, and we've met before. I just can't remember when, or why.'

'I'm Ralph Ireton, from the office of the County Sheriff, and I'm here to advise you that you've been suspended from office.'

'That doesn't particularly surprise me,' Tom grunted. 'Who was it what complained, and have you got any intention of listening to my side of things?'

'The complaint is two-fold,' Ireton explained. 'First of all a complaint of dereliction of duty from a Master Hoskins, who asserts that for two days you declined to investigate a charge of theft by his apprentice.'

'Hoskins is a trouble-making, loud-mouthed, bullying old pisspot,' Tom growled.

'Yes, he spoke highly of you too,' Ireton replied, to appreciative titters from the men around him.

'And more to the point,' Tom added hotly, 'I've just come from talking to the lad what's supposed to have stolen from him.'

'But you don't have him in custody,' Ireton pointed out, and Tom smiled. 'Because the lad's innocent. Hoskins was lying.'

'That's for a court to decide, or did you regard yourself as a judge and jury as well as a Constable?' Ireton grinned. 'That probably explains the second source of complaint – taking it upon yourself to investigate crimes, and interfering with the natural process of these things.'

'Coroner Greville?' Tom enquired, and Ireton nodded. 'Since you were clearly expecting that complaint, presumably I need not acquaint you with its content?'

'He no doubt complained that I caused a delay in an inquest he were pretending to conduct, when the wrong man were about to be sent for trial, just so he could get his supper on time. It just so happens that I'm preparing for the truth to come out, in my capacity as a resident of the county.'

'Not any more you're not,' Tom was assured. 'Not while misusing your powers as a Constable, anyway. Step down from that horse, put it back in the stable, and hand over your staff of office.'

Tom did as requested, after assuring Ireton that the second horse was his, and made his way back into the constables' room in the Guildhall on the pretence that he had some personal items to collect. Giles Bradbury looked up from his desk, his face a picture of embarrassment. 'It weren't me, honest!' he assured Tom, who smiled encouragingly.

'I know who it were, right enough, and now I'm even more determined to prove one of them wrong, and the other one guilty of murder. But first I need you to turn your back for a minute, while I gets something out the cupboard.'

'You're suspended from duty,' Bradbury objected, 'and it's more than my job's worth to let you into that cupboard.'

'And how do you know I'm suspended, when I didn't know myself until a few minutes ago, outside there? And I didn't tell you anything about that, did I?'

'No, but the Sheriff's men come in here, and said they was looking for you, to suspend you from duty.'

'But you didn't know for certain that they had, did you? Now shut your noise, and get your head back into them papers, while I gets what I needs from that cupboard.'

Giles did as instructed, and Tom swiftly removed the ribbon that had been around Amy's neck when she was murdered, the brooch that Tom had found in the grass at the old priory, and the bag of jewels given to him by Hoskins. He tucked them all into his jacket and sauntered out with a cheery farewell to Giles, and an instruction to keep his seat warm until his undoubted return.

He would need to act quickly, before word of his suspension reached the ears of their neighbours in the town, and in particular the Hoskins family. But he also needed to secrete away the vital pieces of evidence that he'd removed from the cupboard, and where better than the overgrown garden about which Lizzie was always complaining, and which even their own children refused to play in any more, preferring the rough open ground a few doors down from the house?

'You decided to plant turnips, or what?' Lizzie demanded as she surveyed him from the rear door of their house. Tom looked up at her and nodded down at the hole in the ground he'd just made with a large stone with a rough edge, into which he'd placed the all-important items before covering the hole over with the aid of his boot heel.

'If you see anyone exploring down here, stop them,' he instructed her sharply, and she burst out laughing. 'You're joking, ain't you? Who'd want to go exploring in that overgrown mess? And apart from leaving your horse to graze in it, you've shown no interest in it yourself in all the years we've lived here, so why now?'

'There's important evidence planted in there,' he advised her. 'Well it's the first thing I've ever known you plant,' she goaded him, 'so it must be important. Now, do you want this here supper or not?'

The next morning he was awoken by Lizzie shaking him roughly by the shoulder, and he opened his eyes to the sight of one of her 'Tell me what's going on, and don't lie to me' faces.

'I just met Martha Collinton in the street. You've been suspended. Why didn't you tell me?'

'I were too busy answering your questions about the garden. Looks like I better get a move on, before it gets to be common knowledge.'

'And where you going at this time of day? Looking for a new job?'

'No, doing my old one. I'm off to see Ellie Hoskins.'

'But you've been suspended!'

'She doesn't know that yet, with a bit of luck. Now, out of my way, because I just got a clever idea.'

He dressed hurriedly and rushed into the garden, where he retrieved the bag of jewels, into which he placed the silver brooch after cleaning it as carefully as he could. Then he saddled the horse and led him into the street, before trotting him the short distance into Pilcher Gate and slipping down from the saddle at the front door of the house next to the tannery. He was about to knock when he heard a woman's voice from the roadway alongside him.

'Constable Lincraft, I believe? Are you seeking Benjamin as usual? And what has the stupid oaf done this time?'

Somewhat taken aback by the woman's polite, educated manner of speech, he turned and smiled. 'Are you by any chance Ellie Hoskins?'

'I'm *Eleanor* Hoskins, certainly,' the woman replied haughtily. 'Only Benjamin insists on lowering me in everyone's eyes by calling me "Ellie". So I repeat – what has he done this time? Or have you perhaps come to return my jewellery, and have you arrested Oswyn Pike?'

Tom smiled, reached into his jacket, and produced the small bag of jewels like a travelling conjurer earning a few pence by entertaining the crowds on market day.

'These are yours, that right?' he enquired innocently, omitting to advise her that all but one of them had been handed to him by her own husband only recently. She examined the contents eagerly, nodding as she identified each item in turn.

'That's my amethyst ring, certainly. And my pearl necklace – not real pearls, obviously, since Benjamin saves the real ones for his lady friends. And you've found my silver brooch! That was the first thing to go missing, and it was given to me by my father for my sixteenth birthday. It has the family crest on it, and is very precious to me – I'm *so* glad it's been found, since it's all I have left to remind me of better days.'

When Tom looked puzzled, she continued.

'My father was Richard Linacre, the brewer. We were quite wealthy, with our own family crest, then he died, and the business failed very quickly. I was reduced to working for a living, maintaining the saddlery owned by my aunt on my mother's side, to which Benjamin used to deliver leather. He was nothing like the man you know – the man you've taken into custody several times. He was handsome, charming, kind, attentive, in fact the exact opposite of what he is now, with his drunken ways and his association with women of quite the wrong sort. And he's not above beating me when in one of his foul moods. But anyway, you don't want my life story, do you? You're only here to return my jewels.'

'So, you have no hesitation in saying that this silver brooch were once yours?' Tom enquired, barely able to contain his excitement, 'and you're sure it went missing before the rest of them jewels?'

'Quite certain – why?'

'Because it's mighty important in a matter that I'm involved with at the moment, and I'll need to keep it, just for a day or two,' Tom advised her as he reached out his hand, and breathed more easily once it was back in his possession.

'When can I claim it back for good?' Eleanor enquired, and Tom gave her a reassuring smile.

'If you come to the Shire Hall on Monday next, the chances are you'll get it back then. Right now, I need to go about my business.'

'No you fucking don't!' came a bellow from the entrance to the tanning yard, and there stood Ben Hoskins, armed with one of the long poles used to stir raw cow hides around in his tanning vat. 'You been suspended, so you've no business asking questions here, or anywhere else! It's the talk of the town that you're not a constable any more, so what you up to, eh? As for you, you useless lump of maggot food,' he yelled across at Eleanor, 'what you been telling him?'

'Nothing!' Eleanor replied with a fearful look. 'He was just returning my jewellery, honestly! I didn't know he wasn't a constable any longer!'

Hoskins glared at Tom. 'If I were you, I'd leave town without further delay, shithead! I'm going to report you to the Sheriff for impersonating a constable, and you'll likely finish up in your own cell, so piss off now, while you can. A long way away, if you knows what's good for you!'

Fortunately Tom was in the process of climbing into the saddle before Eleanor spoke again in her eagerness to appease Ben's wrath.

'There's no harm done, and at least I got all my jewellery back. Even that lovely silver brooch that my father gave me all those years ago. Although Tom Lincraft's taken it back again – claims he needs it for evidence or something.'

The look on Hoskins's face was that of a pole-axed calf in a slaughterhouse as Tom allowed himself the luxury of a rude gesture in his direction before cantering off down Pilcher Gate on his way out of town.

'I've got all the evidence I'm going to need,' Tom told those gathered around him in the estate kitchen, while the Cook served them all bread and cheese. Jane Netherfield had just arrived on her husband's horse, having been summoned by Bessie Helms when Tom first arrived. Bessie had run excitedly all the way to the Netherfield farm, and had travelled back perched on the mount's neck, but she seemed not to be lacking reserves of energy as she snuggled as close to Oswyn Pike as she could get while they all sat around the big table.

'So why do you need us?' Oswyn enquired suspiciously, and Tom's reply was 'Because each of you can supply a little bit of the whole story. Jane can tell the Coroner that the neckband on the body what we found in the paddock were made by her as a present for Amy. That proves that the body were likely Amy's, as far as anything can. Then Bessie tells the jury all about Amy's new rich feller what she were bragging about, and how she probably set out to meet him that day when she never come back. Wednesday – her day off, and her day for meeting her rich feller. She can tell us his name, as well – "Benjamin". And the fact that he had a leather business, and that Amy were going to try and get money out of him on the day when she set out to meet him.'

'I hope I can remember all that,' Bessie whispered apprehensively, and Tom smiled back at her reassuringly. 'Remember that she were your friend – all of you – and that this will be the only chance you have of sending the feller what who killed her to the gallows.'

'She weren't *my* friend,' Oswyn objected, and it was his turn to get a confident smile from Tom. 'Neither were Ben Hoskins,' Tom reminded him, 'But it's you that can tell the jury how he were often out late on Wednesday evenings. And how he come back all flustered one Wednesday night, then disappeared in his wagon the next night, probably carrying a spade.'

'It sounds as if you're leaving it all to us,' Jane objected, 'and how do we know that the Coroner will listen to what we have to tell him?'

'As far as that goes, he won't have any choice,' Tom replied with yet another smile, 'because he's obliged to listen to any evidence that can be made forthcoming in the matter. That's the law.'

'But how does any of this prove who it was that killed poor Amy?' was Jane's next objection, and Tom tapped his nose conspiratorially as he reached into his jacket and extracted the silver brooch. 'That's my job. Now, which of you wants to tell the Coroner that Amy always wore this brooch when she were going out for the day all dressed up?'

'I can do that,' Bessie confirmed gleefully, 'but how does it prove anything about who killed her?'

'Because I can prove who gave it to her in the first place,' Tom beamed back at them all. 'Ben Hoskins were a bit too clever for his own good when he tried to accuse Oswyn of stealing his wife's jewels, just so he had an excuse to get rid of him. Ben knew that Oswyn could tell all about the two late nights and the spade, which is why he had to get him out of the way, before I went asking questions.'

'I'm glad you brought him here,' Bessie gushed as she leaned over and kissed Oswyn on the cheek. 'But how does we get to the town in time for next Monday?'

'In the Master's coach,' Tom advised them. 'Before coming out here, I called into the County Gaol to see him, and he wrote a note what orders the Steward that you're to be allowed to use the coach to come into town on Sunday. And that I'm to be given the money for you all to stay in a decent inn on Sunday night. I'll come and get you from there on Monday morning, and take you all to the inquest.'

'So who *did* give the brooch to Amy?' Bessie persisted, 'and how can you prove who it were?'

'That's going to be the tricky bit,' Tom admitted. 'But be ready when I come up on Sunday to follow your coach into town.'

He had one final matter to attend to before he could go home for supper. He presented himself at the Senior Turnkey's desk in the front entrance to the Guildhall and asked to speak urgently to Constable Bradbury. Giles appeared, somewhat reluctantly, and gave Tom an awkward grin.

'I'll take a guess that you're going to ask me to do something I shouldn't,' he muttered, and Tom gave him a reassuring smile.

'Depends how seriously you takes your job, don't it? I want Ben Hoskins arrested for murder sometime on Sunday. And at the same time I want you to lock up his wife on suspicion of being his accomplice, and to bring her to the inquest on Monday in the Shire Hall.'

Chapter Eight

The courtroom was even more crowded than it had been on the first day, as Tom led his witnesses towards the side bench. Coroner's Clerk Matthew Barton gave a startled squawk and bustled across to challenge them with a testy 'We haven't summoned any more witnesses for today!'

'Maybe *you* haven't,' Tom replied with a smirk, 'but I spent the week doing your job for you. And the purpose of an inquest is to get to the truth. So, you just sit quiet in your corner over there, and let's get to the truth. Not *your* version of it, of course, nor the version what the Coroner thought he were getting, but the *real* truth.'

Barton scuttled away through the back door to warn Sir Henry Greville that the adjourned inquest looked like taking up more than the hour or so that they'd anticipated, and Tom smiled down reassuringly at the nervous looking group on the witness bench.

'You'll be fine, so don't worry. Leave the fancy lawyer arguments to me, and just remember what it is that the jury over there needs to hear.'

He'd spent the whole of the previous day – Sunday – taking his witnesses through what each of them had to advise the Coroner's jury, first of all in the kitchen at Lenton Gregory before they'd taken the coach down into town, then again in an upstairs room of The Bell, where they were all accommodated overnight. Tom had picked them up there in the morning, and guided coachman Jim Batley through the market place, then down Bridlesmithgate and along High Pavement until they reached the Shire Hall.

There was a slight commotion as Giles Bradbury led Eleanor Hoskins into the courtroom with her hands tied together, and with a resentful look on her face. As they came up to the witness bench she gave Tom a frosty look. 'Was this really necessary?' she enquired, and Tom nodded. 'We wanted to make sure you turned up to say your little piece. All we need is for you to tell the Coroner that this here silver brooch were once yours.'

'And that will prove that my pig of a husband murdered his latest fancy woman, as I understand it?'

'How did you know that?' Tom enquired with a puzzled frown, to which she replied 'You'll hear soon enough. Then you'll hear something you probably *didn't* want to hear, regarding whether or not Benjamin Hoskins goes to the gallows.'

Tom looked enquiringly at Giles Bradbury, who shrugged his shoulders dismissively.

'There were no sign of Ben Hoskins at his house, so he must have run off. No doubt this lady played a part in that, so make sure that she don't take them ropes off her wrists. I'll be in the back of the courtroom, just in case.'

Any further conversation was cut short by the entry of the Coroner, who threw himself angrily onto his seat on the bench, then called out loudly for 'Thomas Lincraft'.

Tom stepped forward to stand in front of Greville, who pierced him with a glare that was no doubt intended to be intimidating. 'What's the meaning of this outrage?' Greville demanded, 'and why are there more witnesses to be heard?' Tom treated him to an oily smirk.

'As you yourself ordered, Coroner, this inquest was adjourned for a week in order for me to get more facts about the dead girl. You'll no doubt be pleased to learn that I've done that, and a good deal more besides. I can now give the jury more idea of who murdered her.'

'And how many witnesses will this involve?'

'There's five in all, Coroner, including me.'

'But you've already given evidence,' Greville objected, 'and the law says that you can't do so twice during the same inquest.'

'Begging your pardon and all that,' Tom smiled mockingly, 'I gave evidence the first time as a Constable. Since you took it upon yourself to have me suspended from duty, I'm not a Constable this morning, and I claim the right to give evidence in my own right, as plain simple "Thomas Lincraft", who's got something to tell the jury that'll help them to get to the truth of the matter.'

'I'm not sure that I can allow that,' Greville insisted as he looked towards the jury bench, where a whispered conversation was going on. After an awkward pause, one of them raised a tentative hand, and Greville nodded. 'What do you wish to say?'

The man cleared his throat and then announced that 'I'm Peter Baker, sir, and I speaks for the rest of the jury when I asks if we could hear what Tom Lincraft has to say. Even if he's *not* a constable any more, we all trust him.'

'Oh, very well,' Greville conceded grumpily. 'Tell us what you've got to waste our time with, Lincraft, and let's get this over before dinner.'

'I were going to be the last to give evidence, Coroner,' Tom advised him, 'since what I has to say will tie together what you'll be hearing from the others.'

'And I suppose you've also organised the order in which we're to hear this additional evidence?' Greville demanded, and Tom nodded. 'With your leave, Coroner, the first one's Jane Netherfield.'

Jane stepped into the spot designated for witnesses, and smiled nervously as the Coroner demanded her personal details.

'Jane Netherfield, sir, wife of George Netherfield, of Sands Farm on the Lenton Gregory estate. I'm aged twenty-seven.'

'And what have you to tell us?' Greville enquired in a tone of voice that suggested that he couldn't care less, but Jane had rehearsed her part well, and she held out her left hand, in which was the blue necktie.

'I was advised by Constable Lincraft, as he then was, that this necktie was found around the throat of the dead girl whose body was dug up on the estate. I can identify it by the embroidery, since I made it, and gave it as a present to a friend of mine who worked on the same estate of Anthony Featherstone. Her name was Amy Brindley, and she worked as a maid in the manor house there.'

Greville glared, first at Tom, then at the jury. 'I suppose that resolves any remaining question regarding the identity of the dead girl. Do you have anything to add, witness?'

'Only that she didn't deserve to die that way,' Jane murmured sadly.

'Very well, you're free to go if you wish, or you can rejoin the others on the witness bench,' Greville conceded, before treating Tom to a sarcastically exaggerated smile and the question 'Who's next?'

Bessie Helms rose shakily to her feet and stood on the spot vacated by Jane. She was visibly trembling as she responded to the first question.

'I'm Bessie 'elms, sir – spelled with a "H" – and I works in the kitchen of the manor house where Squire Featherstone's the Master. I knew Amy Brindley, what were a friend of mine, in a manner of speaking, and I know as how she'd lately got herself a new gentleman friend.'

'By all accounts she had plenty of those,' Greville muttered loudly in an audible aside to the jury. 'Was there one in particular that you were aware of?'

'Yes, sir – one by the name of "Benjamin", what were wealthy, and owned a leather business here in the town.' She broke off briefly when a derisive snort could be heard from Eleanor Hoskins, which was silenced by a glare from the Coroner. When Bessie appeared to have fallen silent, Greville urged her on with 'What about this wealthy gentleman friend, witness?'

'Well, sir,' Bessie continued, 'she were in the habit of meeting him in the ruins of the old priory, and . . . . '

'For the purposes of whoring?' Greville demanded, and Bessie shook her head. 'I'm not sure why she were meeting with this "Benjamin", sir, but . . . . '

'It's been well established that the girl was a whore, witness, so don't try to deny it. She may have once been your friend, but she's dead now, so no harm can come to her reputation any longer. Let's just agree that she was in the habit of meeting this mysterious "Benjamin" fellow for the purpose of whoring, although more's the pity that she chose to do so in what was once a fine house of God that now lies in ruins due to poor counsel given to our former King. So, we now know that her latest customer was called "Benjamin", and that he worked in the leather trade. Is there anything else, witness?'

'Quite a bit, sir, if you'll pardon my continuing,' Bessie

persevered as she held out her hand and unclenched her fingers to display the silver brooch. 'Not long before she died, Amy took to wearing this silver brooch what she said had been given her by this man called Benjamin. She were wearing it the last time I saw her, pinned to the blue dress what she always liked to wear for best. She were off to meet this here Benjamin feller, except this time things wasn't so rosy between them, and she were fixing on giving him the "goodbyes". Only she were also going to ask him for more money, see, else she were going to spread bad stories about him in the town here.'

'Disgraceful!' Greville spluttered. 'Little wonder the cunning whore got herself killed! Although that hardly excuses the man himself – this "Benjamin" person – from associating with her. However, it begins to look as if the blame for the death may lie outside the Featherstone estate. And take that smirk off your face, Lincraft! Anything else, witness?'

'No, sir – except the dead girl were my friend.'

'Well, hopefully you've learned to be more discerning over your choice of friends. You may resume your seat, witness. Now then, Master Lincraft, who's next, and why is that lady sitting with her wrists tied?'

'For reasons that will emerge in a short while, Coroner,' Tom replied brusquely. 'The next witness is Oswyn Pike, if you please.'

Oswyn looked down at the floor as he was glared at by Greville, who barked at him as he demanded his name, age and occupation.

'I'm Oswyn Pike, sir, I'm nineteen years old, and I'm a gardener.'

'And why are you here?'

'I used to be apprenticed to Ben Hoskins, sir. In the tanning trade, it were.'

'And?'

'And well, he went and dismissed me for stealing, except I didn't.'

'Stealing what, exactly?'

'Jewels, sir. His wife's. Except I didn't.'

'And what has this to do with the dead girl, unless one of those jewels was the silver brooch that was being worn by the dead girl when she was last seen?'

'It weren't, sir, because I never stole owt – honest!'

Greville allowed himself a loud theatrical sigh for the benefit of the jury, then glared down at Oswyn.

'I may be missing something important here, witness, which means that the jury probably are as well, but what can you possibly tell us that has to do with the death of a girl we now believe to have been Amy Brindley?'

'I were dismissed for nowt, sir.'

'So you said already, and this is getting very tiresome.'

'Tell him *why* you were dismissed,'' Tom whispered hoarsely from his seat on the witness bench, earning himself a ferocious look from Greville. 'Let the witness speak for himself, Lincraft – you'll get your turn in a minute, if we ever get past this dithering boy.'

'I were dismissed for what I knew about Master Hoskins, sir,' Oswyn yelled desperately, and Greville nodded. 'We're finally getting somewhere, if God is on our side. What was it you knew about this Master Hoskins?'

'That he were staying out late every Wednesday night, and he blamed me for misplacing a spade, except I didn't.'

'Let's start with the bit about Wednesday nights,' Greville sighed, and Oswyn now had the bit between his teeth.

'Well, sir, every Wednesday he'd set off on his wagon on the pretence of going to Derby or somewhere to get cow hides for tanning. But he never once come back with any, and the business were fading fast, because he weren't selling any leather goods neither, see?'

'So your employer's business was in a bad way, and he was pretending to travel to an adjoining town to purchase more hides. Was he not simply seeking to preserve his pride, and pretending that his trade was still thriving?'

'But why did he need a spade, sir?'

'Ah yes, the spade,' Greville repeated as he rolled his eyes in a theatrical gesture towards the jury, some of whom smiled, and all of whom were wondering where this was all leading. 'Do *please* tell us about the spade, since we're all agog to learn about it.'

'Well, it were like this. There were one Wednesday night when he come back real late while I were lying awake in my bed above the stables, and it were after that when I heard him stabling the horse and cursing about something or other. He did a lot of cursing, did the Master.'

'What was he cursing about?'

'No idea, but the next night he were off out again.'

'And this would have been a Thursday – not your master's normal night for going out?'

'No – that were the point. Then the next morning I found the spade we used for shifting cow shit lying in the bottom of his wagon. He blamed me for it being there, but the day before I'd left it against the side of the tanning shed, like I normally did. And that's it, really.'

'That's *what* precisely, witness? What on earth has this got to do with the dead girl?'

'Well, just that Ben Hoskins took a spade with him when he went out on the Thursday night, and he knew that I knew, and that's why he dismissed me on a false charge of stealing his wife's jewels.'

Greville shook his head as he ordered Oswyn back to his seat, then glared at Tom.

'I hope your next witness makes more sense, Lincraft.'

'So do I, Coroner,' Tom replied with an exaggerated smile, 'since it's me.'

'What about the lady with her hands tied in front of her?'

'She'll be giving her evidence after me, sir. But since you expressed your confusion and displeasure, a moment ago, regarding how all these bits of evidence fits together, I thought I might oblige the court with an account of the enquiries I spent the past week following up.'

'Enquiries you were not authorised to make in your capacity as a County Constable,' Greville reminded him, and Tom smirked as he replied 'Which makes it perhaps as well that you made sure I were dismissed from that office, so that I could continue to ask questions like any ordinary person. And I got some answers for the jury to listen to.'

'Oh, very well. But get on with it, because the morning's slipping away from us.'

'Well, sir,' Tom began, 'as you'll have gathered, the first thing I did was try to find out who the dead girl were, since we'd had to put off this inquest to find out. We'd all been assuming that it were Amy Brindley, but there were no proof of that. Anyway, I went to the Featherstone estate, and I spoke to the witness Jane Netherfield, who told me about the blue necktie she'd made for the lass Amy. I remembered that there'd been a blue necktie round the neck of the dead girl – in fact, it looked as if it had been used to strangle her.'

He was obliged to pause at this point when Jane Netherfield gave a light squeal and burst into floods of tears. Bessie Helms put her arm around her in a consoling gesture, while Eleanor Hoskins managed to extract a kerchief from her bodice, which she held out awkwardly in her roped hands. Bessie gave her a whispered thanks, and passed it on to Jane, who blew her nose loudly, then gave a bubbling apology to Greville for the interruption. Greville nodded his acknowledgement, then called for Tom to continue.

'Well, once Jane Netherfield had identified the necktie, and it seemed to be proved that the dead girl were indeed Amy Brindley, I asked around the estate regarding the girl's habits. It were Bessie Helms what told me that the lass had a lot of gentlemen friends . . . '

'She was a whore, you mean!' Greville corrected him loudly, and Tom inclined his head in silent agreement. 'She were certainly intending to seek a large sum of money from her latest admirer, and it may be that's what led to whoever it were doing her in. I were also told by staff on the estate that her favourite place of assignation with her latest gentleman – who she told Bessie Helms were called "Benjamin" – were the old priory down the road a bit, on the other side of Lenton Lane. So, I went looking down there, and found that silver brooch lying in the grass just outside where the monks used to have their bedrooms. The way it were lying gave me the idea that maybe it got lost when Amy were struggling with whoever killed her, or maybe when her dead body were being taken away to be buried in the field on the Featherstone estate. And that's something else, by the way.'

'Please don't change the subject at this point,' Greville instructed him. 'Come back to the point about the burying of the body later, if you must. But what about the brooch?'

'Well, I'd already been told by Bessie Helms that the lass Amy had been given it by this feller called "Benjamin", who were in the leather trade somewhere here in the town. So, I took the brooch back to the estate, and Bessie said that right enough, it were the brooch in question. So now I knew I were looking for a feller called "Benjamin" what had a leather business here in the town, who'd given Amy that brooch during one of their meetings.'

'And did you find him?' Greville enquired, now apparently absorbed by what Tom was advising the inquest.

'I reckon so,' Tom smiled. 'It just so happened that Benjamin Hoskins, what owned a tanning business a few streets away from where I live, were demanding that I arrest his apprentice for stealing jewels from Ben's wife. This were Oswyn Pike, as you knows, and when I found him at the place he'd run away to, he told me all about Ben Hoskins's night-time movements, and the business with the spade.'

'Are we talking about the same Benjamin Hoskins who gave evidence, on the first day of this inquest, about having seen the ghost of the girl Amy, who'd told him where to dig for her body?'

'The very same, sir, and you'll recall as how I weren't prepared to believe in all that nonsense about ghosts. But Ben Hoskins were right about where the body were buried, so how did he know? There were one other possible reason for that, and then the lad Pike told me about the business with the missing spade. He also told me something he didn't get round to telling us this morning – do you want him back as a witness?'

'No, God forbid!' Greville replied hastily. 'Just tell us what he told you.'

'Well, sir, he said that on the day Hoskins claims to have seen the ghost, he set off late for what he claimed were another trip to Derby. And you'll recall that Hoskins told this inquest that he were on his way *back* from there when he saw the ghost. Well, the lad Pike told me that it used to take him fours there and four hours back, so the times didn't fit. It were only the middle of the afternoon when Hoskins come back inter town with the story about the ghost, so where had he *really* been? And it were then that I learned that Hoskins had a spade.'

'Perhaps you can now tell us what you learned about the site of the girl's grave, since we've got to that part,' Greville suggested. 'The "something else", as you called it earlier.'

'Ah yes, that,' Tom smiled. 'You remember as how, on the first day of this inquest, the Featherstone estate gardener – Amos Bridges – said he'd seen his master Anthony Feathertsone digging under the same oak tree where the body were found? Well, naturally, I enquired of Featherstone himself about that, and he told me that he'd been digging on another side of the old oak from where the body were, and that he'd been burying something precious in a tin box. I borrowed a spade and dug where he told me, and sure enough there were a tin box, right where he said I'd find it, so that put him in the clear so far as concerns the digging.'

'And what was in the box?' Greville enquired eagerly, but Tom shook his head. 'I never opened it, sir.'

'But where is it now?'

'In the Guildhall, locked away safe in a cupboard where we keep items of evidence.'

Greville seemed disappointed with the answer, but was equally anxious to move matters on.

'Coming back to your earlier evidence, witness – this brooch that you believe may have been worn by the dead girl at the time when her body was being moved. Did you ever find out who its owner was?'

'I did indeed, sir, and it's this final lady who'll be giving evidence. She's Hoskins's wife Ellie, sir.'

'*Eleanor!*' the lady in question shouted indignantly by way of correction. Greville nodded. 'She's your final witness, you say? And all she'll be doing is identifying this silver brooch in front of me here on the bench? If so, we'll take her evidence now, even though it means that dinner will be a little late. Perhaps it would be easier, and a little more dignified, were you to remove her wrist restraints. This is all assuming that you've finished your own evidence, of course.'

A minute later Eleanor Hoskins was standing in the witness space, rubbing at her wrists where they'd been chafed by the ropes. She announced her name, and the fact that she was married to Benjamin Hoskins, then gave her age as thirty-seven.

'Mrs Hoskins,' Greville said in a tone of respect that had not been bestowed on any of the previous witnesses, 'I'm advised that you can identify this brooch as yours – is that correct?'

'It is,' Eleanor replied calmly, and Greville continued in the same tone.

'Do I take it from what we heard earlier that you believed this brooch to have been stolen from you by the witness Oswyn Pike?'

'That was what my husband told me, and I had no reason to believe otherwise. But I now know that he gave it as a gift to his latest whore, and that it somehow got lost in the long grass while he was carrying her body to his wagon after he killed her.'

Greville raised his hand in a silencing gesture.

'That's only conjecture on your part, surely? Certainly, the evidence we've heard this morning might give rise to that inference, but you can't know for certain, can you?'

'Oh yes I can,' Eleanor replied defiantly. 'Because he confessed it all to me. Just before I killed him.'

Chapter Nine

In the stunned silence that followed Eleanor's revelation, a few sharp intakes of breath could be heard from the jury benches, and Greville's mouth opened and closed several times before he found the words.

'You're prepared to admit to having killed your husband, say you?'

'I'm actually quite proud of it,' Eleanor replied calmly, 'and the world's a better place without him.'

Greville gestured with his hand for Tom to step forward again, and nodded towards Eleanor, as she stood silently before the bench. 'Perhaps this woman should be restrained with ropes again, Constable.'

'I'm not a constable no more, remember?' Tom smirked back, 'but Constable Bradbury's somewhere in court, so he can take care of that.'

Once the ropes were back around Eleanor's wrists, Greville demanded that she explain her extraordinary confession in more detail, and she smiled as she duly obliged.

'When Constable Lincraft left our house that morning, after telling me that he'd found my silver brooch, my husband Benjamin seemed like a man in the grip of some sort of seizure. He was trembling, and white in the face. I asked him what was wrong, and he responded by ordering me into the house. I was concerned that this might foretell another beating, so I hid a knife in the folds of my gown. A few minutes later he came into the house, and demanded – Benjamin never "asked" for anything, he always demanded – that I lie about the brooch.'

'He wanted you to deny that it was yours?' Greville enquired, but Eleanor shook her head. 'No, he wanted me to say that I'd actually seen Oswyn Pike slipping it into his jacket, but I refused. I said that it wouldn't be fair to accuse the boy in that way, and perhaps have him falsely imprisoned, and then Benjamin told me that he'd given the brooch to his latest whore – although he didn't quite put it in those terms – and that the girl had died accidentally when they'd been struggling. I asked what they'd been struggling about, and where, and Benjamin told me that they'd been down at the old priory, and that the girl had threatened to accuse him of raping her.'

'So, the girl was killed by accident?' Greville enquired, but Eleanor shook her head.

'So Benjamin tried to insist, to begin with. But then I asked him why he'd been with the girl in such an isolated place in the first place, and accused him of whoring with her. He became quite angry, and shouted that she'd been worse than a whore, and she deserved to die for trying to extract money from him. I told him that I didn't believe that she'd died by accident, and that I had no intention of risking being sent to prison for lying to the authorities about his involvement in the girl's death. Then he began raving and shouting that he'd "choked the daylights out of the little harlot" – his words, not mine – and that he'd do the same to me if I didn't help him to cast the blame on Oswyn Pike. I unwisely replied that Oswyn Pike was a better person that he was, and that I wouldn't tell a lie that would see him hang, and that's when Benjamin flew at me and tried to strangle me to death. God must have been by my side when he urged me to arm myself with that knife, and you'll find Benjamin's body in the shit pile at the back of the house, where it belongs. "Ashes to ashes, dust to dust, and shit to shit", as far as I'm concerned. You can take me away now, if that's the appropriate procedure.'

In what seemed like a dream, Tom stepped forward instinctively, then stepped back, red-faced, when he remembered that he was no longer authorised to take criminals into custody, and watched as Giles Bradbury led Eleanor out of the courtroom, after allowing himself a sly wink in Tom's direction. As Eleanor disappeared from sight behind the double doors that led into the corridor, Greville seemed to start from a reverie of his own, and turned to address the jury.

'Would I be right in thinking that you have heard enough to enable you to bring in a true verdict in the matter with which you were originally charged, before this amazing turn of events?'

There was an excited murmuring between the twelve men,

before the one they had elected as their spokesman on the first day replied 'We have, Coroner, and we have a verdict.'

'Proceed, and my clerk will record it,' Greville instructed them, and the spokesman - elected since he was the only literate one amongst them - rose to his feet, held up the piece of paper that contained the outline of what he had to say, and announced that 'We, the members of the jury called to enquire into the circumstances leading to the discovery of the body of a female in Lenton Gregory on the third day of July in this year of 1571 find that the body was that of one Amy Brindley, maidservant of one Anthony Featherstone, and that she was killed feloniously by the hand of one Benjamin Hoskins of Nottingham on some date prior to the said third day of July.'

Greville frowned at the spattering of applause that rippled through the courtroom following this pronouncement, then fixed Tom with another of his steely glares.

'That no doubt brought you a great deal of somewhat unnecessary satisfaction, Master Lincraft, but I shall ensure that the thorough investigation that you conducted into this case is reported to the Sheriff of Nottinghamshire, and no doubt the miscarriage of justice that led to your suspension from your duties as Constable will be overturned in due course.'

'Talking of miscarriages of justice,' Tom replied with a broad smile, 'will you now order the release, of Anthony Featherstone, without any more delay? 'He's spent too long down below here already.'

'Yes, of course. And now let's all adjourn for dinner.'

As Greville rose from the bench and lumbered back through the door to his private chamber, Tom turned to look back smilingly at his witnesses, and was almost knocked flat as they ran to embrace him, thank him and congratulate him on his triumph. They insisted on all but dragging him down Stoney Street to the 'Old Angel', where they celebrated with ale, bread and cheese, using up the remainder of the money entrusted to them by the estate Steward for their accommodation. Much later that afternoon Tom looked over the top of his fourth mug of ale to see Lizzie standing in the doorway in her customary battle pose, hands on hips.

'They told me I'd find you in here' she frowned. 'I don't think you'll need any supper after this lot, so if you can find your own way home when the ale runs out, you'll find me with my feet up, enjoying a snooze.'

'I obviously can't thank you enough,' Anthony Featherstone beamed as he raised his brandy goblet in a salute to Tom, 'and you, Mrs Lincraft, must be exceedingly proud to have such a God-fearing and honest man for a husband.'

'He has his moments,' Lizzie acknowledged gruffly.

'And this was undoubtedly one of them, for which I shall remain eternally grateful,' Anthony smiled.

They were spending the weekend as Anthony's honoured guests on his estate, and had just finished an excellent dinner. Robert and Lucy had been sent to explore the grounds under the supervision of Amos Bridges, and the adults were relaxing in front of the log fire that had just been lit against the encroaching dampness of the early Autumn afternoon. They would be returning home the following day, after a hearty breakfast, in the same estate coach that had brought them from Barker Lane earlier that day, and Tom would be returning to duty on Monday morning, reinstated to his former duties, but with the rank of 'Senior Constable' that the County Sheriff had insisted upon, much to Greville's chagrin, when news reached his office of the exemplary investigation conducted by Tom that had narrowly avoided a horrible miscarriage of justice.

'What will happen to poor Mrs Hoskins?' Anthony enquired sadly, but Tom smiled back reassuringly. 'She likely won't hang, anyway. For one thing she did us all a kindness by ridding the town of one of its worst, and for another she did what she did to defend her own life. I reckon she'll be released to live what's left of her life as a widow woman.'

'Talking of happy endings,' Anthony smiled, 'it looks as if I've acquired a successor to old Amos when he retires. He speaks highly of his new assistant, young Oswyn, and to judge by the attention he's receiving from the girl Bessie in the kitchen we're likely to have a married couple living above the stables before too much longer. But what I can't understand,'

Anthony continued as he swirled his brandy around in its goblet, 'is why the man Hoskins was so stupid as to draw attention to the existence of the body. It could have lain there forever, and none of us any the wiser.'

'Probably not,' Tom replied. 'I seem to remember that you use that bottom paddock for winter bedding for the horses in the stable, right?'

'Yes, but so what?'

'When does you harvest it?'

'Early Autumn, while it's still turning brown, and is long enough to make decent stall bedding. In fact, we'll be making a start on it in a few weeks' time.' Then the realisation hit him, and he smiled. 'Of course, it might have been noticed then that there was something different about the patch where the girl was buried.'

'Also the patch where you buried them papers,' Tom reminded him. 'I can keep them for you for a while if you like.'

'Yes, that might be best,' Anthony agreed. 'But I hope you didn't have to tell a lie about them to the Coroner.'

'No,' Tom grinned, 'When he asked me what were in the box, I just told him I hadn't opened it, which were true.'

'All the same,' Anthony smiled in a mocking expression of disapproval, 'you must say an additional prayer for forgiveness at our next meeting. But surely the man Hoskins had nothing to gain by having the body discovered earlier than it might otherwise have been? He was simply drawing attention to himself in the most unbelievable of ways, with all that nonsense about a ghost.'

'It's nonsense to you and me, because we follow the true faith, but there was plenty of others what was prepared to believe it. Even Lizzie here, though she won't admit it now.'

'Leave me out of this,' Lizzie insisted as she smiled lovingly at Tom anyway.

'And,' Tom added, 'we got lucky that Hoskins just panicked when he did, and thought that maybe by making himself the one what drew attention to the body, he'd be the last person to be suspected. We constables rely a good deal on folks like Hoskins being stupid. That's how we catch most of them, even though we're not supposed to go investigating the way I did.'

'Well,' Anthony smiled as he raised his glass, 'Here's to Senior Constable Lincraft catching many more stupid criminals, even if he breaks the odd rule in the process.'

'So long as he don't finish up as stupid as them,' Lizzie added with a smile.

On the Monday morning a small crowd of Guildhall staff had gathered to cheer Tom back to duty, and he was handed a mug of ale by a grinning Giles Bradbury. The two men made their way into the inner office once the others had begun to drift back to their various duties, and Giles shook his head in quiet disbelief.

'Just to think that a week ago you were suspended from duty, and now you're back in here, promoted to "Senior Constable". But you deserve it, and I has to admit that you put up quite a show at that inquest – better than some lawyers I've seen.'

'I had to break a few rules, remember,' Tom reminded him. 'Don't go picking up my bad habits.'

'But how can they be said to be bad, if you gets the right result in the end?' Giles argued. 'If it hadn't been for you poking and prying where you shouldn't, poor old Anthony Featherstone would be on his way to the gallows. That's why I took this job – to see justice being done to the right folks for the right reason.'

'Me too,' Tom admitted with a rueful grin. 'But as you can see from what happened to me, you're in danger of treading on the wrong toes sometimes.'

'I'd like to work with you on your next matter, if that'd be acceptable to you,' Giles said with a sheepish grin. 'I wants to learn how to do things the way you do.'

An hour later he got his wish. There was a sharp thump on the door, and the Chief Turnkey poked his head round after opening it with obvious urgency.

'Tom, there's a feller out here what reckons he's just found his father hanging from a roof beam in the mill he owns down by Leenside. Could you look into it?'

'Tell the man we'll be right out,' Tom assured him, then caught the smile on Giles's face.

'Well, you said you wanted to learn from me, didn't you? Off your arse, and let's go and risk being bitten by rats.'

Endnote

It's a truism that novelists should write about things with which they are familiar, and after half a lifetime working as a public prosecutor my familiarity with the lives and work of senior police officers brought Detective Chief Inspector Mike Saxby to life with ease. I also recall that, like the rest of us, they have private lives and families. But, unlike the rest of us, the two often conflict, as I hope I have underlined in this first novel in the series. Likewise, in the next, 'Justice Delayed', we get to learn what drives the somewhat crumpled and dishevelled DI Dave Petrie, as well as delving further into the researches conducted by investigative journalist Jeremy Giles, whose murder becomes the focus of Mike Saxby's next enquiry.

My creation of the fictional 'Brampton' will fool nobody resident in Nottingham, given the occasional references to its location, but again I was writing about a place I know well, while availing myself of the freedom to describe settings such as the police headquarters and the layout of a North Midlands English city. I hope I will be forgiven this little subterfuge, and that you were sufficiently drawn into the professional and personal lives of the characters to want to read more. I would particularly value your feedback on this new project of mine, either by way of reviews on Amazon or Goodreads, or more directly on my website page, davidfieldauthor.com. I look forward to hearing from you, and thank you for taking the time to read this book.

David

*

Printed in Poland
by Amazon Fulfillment
Poland Sp. z o.o., Wrocław

58787511R00059